She cou ~~~~~ **etts needed her help.**

"I ride a horse for a living," Violet said by way of answering. "Next to controlling a thousand pounds of stubborn muscle, not much intimidates me. Least of all working with you."

"Glad to hear it." Boone smiled. He had one of those smiles that was clearly hard-won, but once he did, it made everyone who saw it grin back.

Including Violet.

She realized she was staring at him, so she dropped her eye contact only to notice huge wet spots all over the legs of his jeans.

Boone glanced down. "Ah, that. On my way in I was hug attacked by two very wet six-year-olds."

Violet chuckled. "They can be a handful."

"At least they're the good kind of handful," Boone joked.

Violet followed him out of the barn and watched him walk away, the whole time wondering what she had gotten herself into.

She hoped, to borrow Boone's words, she was about to be busy with the good kind of handful.

Avid reader, coffee drinker and chocolate aficionado **Jessica Keller** has degrees in communications and biblical studies and spends too much time on Instagram and Pinterest. Jessica calls the Midwest home. She lives for fall, farmers' markets and driving with the windows down. To learn more, visit Jessica at www.jessicakellerbooks.com.

Visit the Author Profile page at Harlequin.com for more titles.

Starting Over in Texas

Jessica Keller

LOVE INSPIRED
INSPIRATIONAL ROMANCE

ISBN-13: 978-1-335-48819-0

Starting Over in Texas

Copyright © 2020 by Jessica Koschnitzky

This edition published by arrangement with Harlequin Books S.A.

For questions and comments about the quality of this book, please contact us at CustomerService@Harlequin.com.

Love Inspired
22 Adelaide St. West, 40th Floor
Toronto, Ontario M5H 4E3, Canada
www.Harlequin.com

Printed in U.S.A.

He healeth the broken in heart,
and bindeth up their wounds.
—*Psalm* 147:3

For Ellie. Thank you for always being excited about my books! I love seeing all the pictures of you reading them. Keep reading, keep growing, keep being kind and keep learning.
But most important, always, always, *always* listen to your mom.
Trust me on this—she's one smart lady.

Chapter One

"That better not be Hailey." Boone Jarrett squinted toward the farthest riding arena as he turned his sedan up Red Dog Ranch's long driveway. Gravel churned under his tires as worry roiled in his gut. Out of habit, Boone reached for the passenger seat, toward where his wife's hand usually rested on her leg. There was nothing.

There never would be again.

His eyes burned and no matter how many times he swallowed, his throat closed up.

June was gone. Forever. With her funeral so fresh in his memory it was a wonder how often he forgot she wasn't there any longer. Just assumed she would be beside him as she always had been. But he would never be able to reach out for her comfort again. His breathing became shallow. If he focused on his grief it would debilitate him. It would swallow him and everything he cared about—including his daughter, Hailey.

Boone refused to allow that to happen.

He forced his body to drag air in through his nose, filling his lungs, then let it out slowly, evenly. *Stay in control.* In the four days it had taken him to drive from Maine to Texas, he had thought everything through. Navigating their loss logically was the only way to help his daughter. The only option if he wanted to keep functioning and to make certain she felt safe. Seeing her father falling apart would do neither of them any good.

Logic had carried him through his last few months of seminary despite his loss; it would have to be enough to get him through the summer as he decided their next steps, too.

After shoving the gearshift into Park, Boone climbed out of the vehicle and stalked toward the arena. Sure enough, that was his six-year-old daughter up on a huge horse—a horse that could buck and send her tiny body flying in the space of a heartbeat.

Way too dangerous.

Sweat touched his brow and his back as his stride ate up the distance to the riding arena. After two years of mild Maine summers, Boone wasn't used to the Texas heat he had known growing up. But presently, with the calendar nearing July, it felt as if the sun had a personal vendetta against him.

Boone picked up his pace. His family had suffered too much loss in the last few years for his daughter to be taking needless risks. His father had been killed when he was struck by a car while returning books to the library, of all things, and his wife had died on a hiking trip with girlfriends.

Hailey didn't belong anywhere near that beast.

Back in seminary, he had once preached a sermon on the topic of anger and how, more often than not, that emotion was the child of a much stronger one: fear. Distantly he remembered the point of the sermon was something about the strength of faith and focusing on Jesus in the midst of fear, but those thoughts gave way when he saw the large horse frog-hop with his tiny child on it. He had grown up around horses on this very ranch, so he knew enough to know that a frog-hop could lead to a lot more than Hailey could handle.

Boone started running. "Get her off that thing. They're not safe."

A woman with long blond hair held the lead line of the horse Hailey was riding. She spun in her boots, quirking an eyebrow as her striking green eyes snapped to meet his. "That *thing* is a horse. And if you're so worried about these 'dangerous beasts'—" she made air quotes for the last two words "—I'm sure hollering around them is definitely the best plan for safety."

A part of Boone knew the wisest course was to back down. His time would be better spent greeting his daughter, whom he hadn't seen in eight weeks. But after being trapped in a car for four days with only his thoughts for company, something about the potential of sparring with this woman made him feel alive. And he hadn't felt that way in a long time, if he was

being honest. Like a valve on a water main, he had
turned his emotions to the Off position since June's
accident. Because he knew when he turned the valve
back on, it would cause a flood. A flood he might not
be able to recover from. He had been functioning on
numb the past few months so in some weird way, it
was nice to feel a flicker of emotion. Any emotion.

"No one asked my permission for Hailey to learn
to ride."

The woman popped a hand to her hip. "See, and
therein lies the main problem here." She pinned
him with a glare. "*You* would have actually had to
be around for us to ask your permission. And you
weren't, were you? Hailey's been alone here for
months without you."

A hot wave of frustration flashed through Boone's
chest. This woman didn't know him. What gave her
the right to speak to him that way? Then again, he
didn't have a leg to stand on when it came to her
point. He hadn't been around. He had left Hailey at
his family's ranch for more than two months while
he was in Maine. But Boone didn't need to explain
himself to some stranger. Besides, even if he wanted
to, he wasn't going to get into those specifics while
his daughter could overhear.

He ran a hand over his close-cropped hair and
looked away. Arguing with this woman would get
him nowhere fast. "Someone could have asked me. I
called here every night. I would have said no to something so dangerous."

She gazed toward the brown horse and snorted. "They're hardly dangerous, especially that oaf."

Boone jabbed his finger toward the horse. "Just last year my niece broke her arm falling off of one. And some barrel racer broke her leg and her horse was injured badly enough to ruin him at an event held here not that long ago too. I heard it was career-ending. So don't tell me they aren't dangerous."

The woman's nostrils flared and her free hand balled into a fist. "Not that you care, but that barrel racer is me." She slammed her palm to her chest. "And as you can see, my leg is just fine." She took a step toward him. "And my career is *far* from over." She made a shooing motion, dismissing him. "So feel free to take your presumptions and march right on out of here. They aren't needed or wanted."

Boone opened his mouth to say something but didn't know exactly how to respond. This was the champion barrel racer? She was younger than his sister, Shannon. She was also incredibly beautiful.

And her glare was hot enough to burn him.

"Daddy!" Hailey's voice finally caught his attention. From her perch on top of the horse, she reached toward him. "You're home."

Boone pulled her from the large horse and gathered his daughter to his chest in a hug. "It's so good to see you." He kissed the top of her head. Her hair was the same exact honey-blond shade his late wife's had been. The thought made Boone's chest ache. "I love you so much."

She looped her arms around his neck. "I missed

you." She tipped her head back a bit to meet his eyes. "But you should be nicer to Violet. She's my friend."

Boone pivoted to see the blonde woman again. Violet. She still looked as if she wouldn't mind seeing a horse kick him more than a few times. He cleared his throat and extended his free hand. "I'm Boone Jarrett."

She pursed her lips and crossed her arms, pointedly ignoring his offered handshake. "I figured as much."

He let his hand drop back to his side. When she didn't supply her last name he said, "I assume you're the famous Violet Byrd?" It had taken a moment of digging through his mental files, but he had finally remembered the name of the champion barrel racer who had once been a camper at Red Dog Ranch.

"She's great," Hailey said. "I love Violet."

Piper, Boone's niece, who was the same age as Hailey, waved at him from on top of her miniature horse. "Hi, Uncle Boone."

"Hey there, sweetheart." He carried Hailey over to where Piper was and patted his niece's head. Double braids went down Piper's back. She had worn her hair that way ever since it had been long enough to make into a braid. Piper swung off her little white horse to hug his leg.

He crouched to meet her, setting Hailey down in the process. "Do you know where your dad or your uncle Rhett is?" Piper's dad was Boone's younger brother, Wade, who was the head of maintenance at

Red Dog Ranch, while Rhett, the eldest Jarrett, was the owner and director.

Hailey touched his arm. "Uncle Rhett is gone away."

"Everyone's sad because of Silas," Piper added.

Boone's stomach clenched, he looked to Violet. Silas was Rhett and Macy's one-month-old son. Violet sighed and nodded slowly. So she knew what they were talking about.

Boone rose. "What's going on?"

Violet glanced at Hailey and Piper. "Could you girls get Sheep's saddle off and make sure his bucket is full of fresh water?" She jutted her chin toward the little white horse. "I'll join you in the barn in just a minute."

Hailey jumped up and down beside her cousin as Piper led Sheep out of the arena. Boone watched the two little girls as they walked away, not exactly happy that Hailey was still involved in something horse-related, but also knowing that whatever Violet wanted to say, she clearly didn't want to say it in front of the girls.

He turned toward her. "What happened?" And why hadn't anyone called him? Why did she know more about his family than he did?

Violet's eyes searched his. "Macy noticed Silas has been having a hard time breathing these last few days, but she wrote that off as being a new mother who worried too much. But this morning his lips and the tips of his fingers started turning blue."

Boone latched his hand onto the nearby fence rail for support. "Blue?"

Every loss, every miscarriage and blow he and June had faced during their years of infertility after having Hailey, crashed through him. He didn't want Rhett to go through the loss of a child. *Dear God, be with them.*

"They rushed him to urgent care," Violet said. "From there he was taken by helicopter to Texas Children's Hospital. Rhett and Macy followed by car. You can image how frantic and upset they are." She wound the large horse's long lead line around in her hand. "I'm sure they mean to call you later when they know more."

Boone's knees felt weak. Not another hit for their family. They couldn't take it. Why did God keep chipping away at the Jarretts? "They took him all the way to Houston?"

She nodded.

"Do they know what's wrong?" Boone prayed for Silas and Rhett and Macy. He prayed for the doctors and nurses at the hospital and he asked God to help get his family through the season of hit after hit they seemed stuck in. Since his wife's death, Boone had been angry at and doubtful of God, but he knew right now prayer and people gifted in the medical field were the two most important things for little Silas. Despite his personal struggles, the only thing Boone knew how to do to help in the situation was pray.

"I don't have the whole story." She grimaced in an apologetic way. "You'll have to ask Wade for the particulars, but Rhett said they were worried about the baby's heart." Violet held up a hand in a don't-freak-out way. "He also said that hospital has one of the best heart centers in the nation." She pointed behind him. "There's Wade now. I'll hang on to Hailey and Piper if you want to talk to him."

"Thank you." Boone spun in the direction she had pointed in and started to walk away.

"And Boone," Violet called from behind him, causing him to look over his shoulder. "Hailey has missed you. She's missed you so much. Two months is a long time for a kid to be away from a parent."

Her words bit with the sting of a riding whip. Boone swallowed past the burning sensation in his throat. "I know. I've missed her, too." Then he turned back around and headed toward Wade.

Boone had greeted Wade with a tight embrace and then they had launched right into talking about baby Silas and everything that was going on. Their brother's newborn needed a new heart. Dilated cardiomyopathy, Wade had said. The condition meant the main chamber of the baby's heart was enlarged and weakened, which was preventing his heart from pumping like it was meant to.

If Silas didn't get a heart transplant in time, the condition would kill him.

Boone tried to make sense of it all as Wade plowed ahead, trying to catch him up.

"I'm going to need your help," Wade said.

"Anything." Of course Boone would help his family. Besides, keeping busy was his favorite way to avoid dwelling on things like loss and worry.

Wade explained Rhett had also started training service dogs and his first dog, a black Lab named Ryker, was fully trained and would be picked up the next day. "Rhett's obviously not here and I have a cattle auction tomorrow so I'm not available," Wade said. "I texted Patrick—he's the dad of Ryker's boy—and he knows to find you to pick up the dog."

"I can do that," Boone said. He glanced back toward the barn.

Wade clasped his shoulder. "Don't worry about our daughters. They love spending time with Violet and she's great with them."

Violet's charged words and accusation about Boone not being around rattled through him. Boone scrubbed at the back of his neck. "She's really made herself at home here in a short amount of time. She knew about Silas before anyone thought to call me."

Wade shook his head. "It's not like that at all. Rhett told us to wait to tell you in person. He didn't want to worry you while you were driving and you were set to arrive today anyway. Violet happened to be nearby when I got the call. She offered to take the girls off my hands so Cassidy and I could take care of things for Rhett."

Boone released a shaky sigh. "Then I guess it's a good thing she's here." Especially since their sister, Shannon, had eloped a few weeks ago and headed with her new husband on a three-month-long veterinary mission trip to South America. Not exactly what

Boone would have chosen to do for a honeymoon; then again, he and June had been too young and too poor to afford a trip at all when they got married.

For so many years the family had always counted on Shannon to pitch in wherever they needed help at the ranch and she had always been happy to provide childcare for her nieces. Boone had to admit, it was kind of Violet to step into that role while their sister was gone.

"Hailey has really taken a liking to Violet," Wade said. He looped his fingers around his belt. "They spend a lot of time together and Violet has a way of connecting with her." He jutted his chin toward the barn. "Honestly, Violet's been a Godsend. Cassidy hasn't been feeling well and I'm determined to be there for her and do whatever she needs every step of this pregnancy. Violet is always willing to take the girls when we ask or when Cassidy needs to rest."

Boone understood Wade's meaning. Wade hadn't been around for Cassidy when she was pregnant with their first child, Piper. In fact, at the time the whole family had thought Wade was dead. Five years after he disappeared, Wade had shown up at the ranch, alive and well, only to learn he had a daughter. Boone knew supporting Cassidy during her second pregnancy meant everything to Wade.

Boone glanced toward the barn and groaned. "I'm afraid Violet and I may not have gotten off on the right foot."

Wade frowned. "What did you do?"

Boone rolled his shoulders. "I only told her I didn't want Hailey learning how to ride a horse."

"Well, it's too late for that." The smile on his brother's face held a note of pride. "Hailey's gotten pretty good at it already. She's catching up to Piper and that's saying a lot. My little lady's been riding since she could walk."

"It's dangerous." Boone was aware of the low grumble in his voice, but couldn't rein it in. He had just lost his wife. He didn't want anything happening to his daughter. Why couldn't anyone understand that?

Wade shrugged. "No more dangerous than driving a car."

"Good thing I'm not letting Hailey do that, either," Boone deadpanned.

Wade rolled his eyes in an annoyingly exaggerated way only a younger sibling could. "You know, if you really did get off on the wrong foot with Violet, you're going to have to extend an olive branch to her."

"I know, I know," Boone said. "She lives here right now and we'll be seeing a lot of each other."

"Not just that," Wade said. "I need you to run the ranch together."

If Wade had told him that he wanted Boone to build an elaborate float and drive it in the Macy's Thanksgiving Day Parade in New York, he wouldn't have been more shocked.

Boone opened his mouth, shut it. "Come again?"

"Silas needs a heart transplant," Wade said each word slowly. "Rhett and Macy will be living at a hotel near the hospital for as long as he's there. That could be weeks, months. Possibly longer. No one knows when or if a heart will become available. But we know for sure they're going to miss the entire summer here. Beyond the health crisis our nephew is facing, you understand the significance of them not being here, don't you?"

Of course Boone did. Rhett and Macy were codirectors of the ranch. They ran…*everything*. And with it being summer, Camp Firefly, the summer camp the ranch hosted at no cost for kids in the foster care system, would already be in full swing.

Boone blew out a long puff of air. "What are you going to do?"

"Actually, the real question is, what are *you* going to do?" Wade pushed his pointer finger into Boone's chest. He continued before Boone could react. "I know you're already facing a lot, but we need you, Boone. This family needs you to step up and run the camp and financial side of the ranch while Rhett is gone."

"I don't think that's a good idea." Boone shook his head. He wanted to help his family, but running the ranch? That was out of his wheelhouse. He had intended to come back to heal around his family, to have time with Hailey and to be away from Maine where they had so many recent memories with June. Boone was supposed to use the summer to decide if he was going to finish seminary. Running the ranch would not help him solve anything. Besides, when their father died, the will had specified that the ranch was to be left to Rhett in full and if the eldest Jarrett didn't want his inheritance then it could pass to Boone or be sold with the proceeds being donated. Boone hadn't wanted to run the ranch then any more than he wanted to do so now. While he loved Red Dog Ranch as his home, his ambitions had always lain elsewhere, which was why he had been attending seminary the last few years. Boone wasn't and never would be a rancher.

"It doesn't matter if it's a good idea," Wade said. "You're all we've got, so you're going to run the show. Case closed."

Boone worked his jaw back and forth. Why did Shannon have to be gone? She would have been perfect for the role. "What about you?"

"I'm already head of maintenance. Do you know how much work it is to maintain over one hundred acres of land and all the machinery and buildings it takes to run this property?" Wade stretched his arms to encompass the expanse of land they owned. "Not just that, I've been running the cattle side of the ranch for the last four months and on top of those things, I've taken over managing all the ranch hands. I also happen to have a pregnant wife and a fairly new marriage I'm trying to keep healthy." He put his hands up in an act of surrender. "My hands are full, buddy. I honestly can't handle anything else."

Boone hadn't comprehended how much his younger brother was already shouldering and felt foolish for having suggested he take on more. He linked his fingers behind his neck and looked out across the pastures. He wanted Red Dog Ranch to be successful because he loved his family and believed in their mission to help foster kids. What kind of minister-in-training would Boone be if he turned his back on his family when they were in need?

Boone sucked in a long breath. "You're right. You have way too much on your plate already." He held up a hand. "Now, I don't know if I know how to do everything. I've been away from the ranch for years. But with some help, I'm willing to try."

Wade smiled. "Like I said before, Violet will help you."

"Violet?" With the amount of information Wade had tossed his way in the last few minutes, Boone hadn't caught that tidbit. "I thought she was working with the horses."

Wade's laugh was rich and a welcome change, given the heavy topics they'd been discussing. "Violet was in a leg cast for seven weeks. She only just got it off. No, she hasn't been working with the horses, not until just this week. But the second they brought her back from the hospital after she was first injured she crutched her way into the office and told Macy to teach her everything because she wanted to be useful and knew Macy was going to have to go on leave soon." Wade gestured to where the ranch office sat at the front of their property, near the driveway. "We had assumed Shannon would fill in at the office while Macy was on maternity leave so after she eloped, we were left scrambling. Macy was only too happy to teach Violet, and Violet's been running the show ever since. Thankfully she seems to have a knack for it."

"You're telling me Violet's been running our family's ranch these last few weeks?"

Wade moved his hand in the universal kinda-sorta motion. "Remember, she spent a good ten or so summers here as a camper so she knows how that part of things goes. And up until today, Rhett's been here. He was tired from having a newborn at home, of course, but he was still around to do most of it with her helping." He thumped Boone's chest. "And now it's all you, bud."

Boone scrubbed his hand over his jaw and faced the barn. "Which means it's olive branch time."

Wade squeezed his shoulder and gave it a little shake. "Sounds about right." He let go. "Send the girls up to the mess hall. Cassidy and I will be in there prepping for tomorrow."

Tomorrow? Right, campers arrived on Sunday afternoons. Apparently his new position started right this minute.

Boone swallowed hard and headed toward the barn.

Violet peeked outside to monitor how Hailey and Piper were doing on the chore she had assigned them. Armed with scrub brushes and a hose, the little girls were tackling a pile of dirty feed buckets. When she spotted them, Violet stifled a laugh. They seemed to be successfully getting more water on each other than the actual buckets, but it was such a hot day and they were young. She could hardly blame them. Kids that age should be allowed to enjoy innocent, carefree fun.

How many times had Violet wished her childhood had been just like that?

She headed back inside the barn and ended up in front of Hawken's stall. Her palomino horse nickered as she approached and stretched so he could rest his head on her back as she trailed her fingers over his neck.

Her horse was injured badly enough to ruin him. Ruin him.

She had tried to block out Boone's hurtful words, but they had rammed back into her mind again and again over the last thirty minutes. Had she ruined Hawken? Only time would tell. So far, he seemed to be doing well, but Shannon's veterinarian husband, Carter, had told Violet it would be at least a year before Hawken could race again—if he was ever strong enough to race again.

Guilt burned a hole through her stomach.

Violet's fingers shook as she continued to pet the gelding. "I'm so sorry," she whispered against Hawken's soft yellow hair. "He was right. You got hurt because I was distracted. It was my fault. You're the best thing—the only good thing—that ever happened to me and I hurt you. I'll never forgive myself for this."

Someone cleared their throat behind Violet and it definitely wasn't one of the girls. Her back went rigid and her hand froze on Hawken. How much had Boone overheard?

"I should have never said those things to you." Boone's shoes crunched on the floor, signaling he had taken a step closer. When she didn't turn to face him, he let out a loud sigh. "I have a lot on my mind right now and Hailey is really important to me and I—"

Violet whirled to face him. "If Hailey is so important to you, why did it take you so long to make your way back to Red Dog Ranch?" Her chest heaved a little. "She should have been your *first* priority." She probably shouldn't keep challenging Boone. He was one of the Jarretts, after all, and if she upset him, he could ask Rhett to toss her off their property and then where would she go?

Violet had spent most of her adult life living out of hotel rooms as she traveled from one rodeo to the next. She had a PO box for legal reasons, but no real home base. She usually found a bedroom to rent near the stables she kept Hawken at in the off season. To her name she had a nice truck and a horse trailer, and the only family she had was Hawken. He was happy to travel anywhere with her. As long as they were together, they were fine. Always had been, always would be. But after his fall, Hawken wouldn't be fit to run the barrels until next summer, and that was only if his leg healed fully.

Violet had just gotten her cast off. Seven weeks in a cast meant muscle loss so she was out of practice, too. Since aging out of the foster system, the rodeo had been her only way of making money. With Hawken hurt, she was stripped of that unless she bought another horse. Beyond that, transporting

Hawken would endanger him. She couldn't do that any more than she could bring herself to replace him with a new horse.

But she also couldn't completely hold her tongue, either.

Boone Jarrett was in the wrong. He had abandoned his daughter mere weeks after her mother had died, which was when Hailey had needed him the most. She knew he had video-chatted with her during his absence, but that wasn't the same as being around and being there for his daughter in the midst of the biggest loss of her life.

A muscle in Boone's jaw ticked. "I don't see why that's any of your business."

Violet spread her fingers over her collarbone. "It's my business when I've held a sobbing six-year-old every day for the past two months because her daddy wasn't there to hug her. It becomes my business when I've had to explain again and again to her that I'm sure her daddy loves her and wants to be here but he can't be."

Boone's whole face fell. There was no other way to describe his expression. "No one told me she's been crying because I wasn't here. I didn't know. She didn't cry during our calls."

Knowing Boone was grieving as well, the rest of the Jarretts had more than likely been trying to protect him. But they should have said something. Hailey had deserved for her father to know she was struggling, and Boone had deserved the chance to make things right.

"Your siblings didn't want to upset you." A twinge of pity caused Violet to soften her tone, but not her message. "You should have known, Boone. A child needs their dad when they're hurting. Of course she was all smiles when you guys talked—she was happy to see you and didn't want to make you sad. But she's been hurting so much and you were the person she needed most of all."

Boone stumbled a little as he reached for the edge of the row of stalls. He braced his hand against it. His head drooped and he closed his eyes as he pinched the bridge of his nose. "I had to finish the semester and close down our life in Maine." A breath rattled out of him. "There were things I needed to take care of but I never meant to hurt her."

Boone was a big guy—wide shoulders and biceps that looked as if he spent hours in the gym. It made her heart do funny things to see such a strong man be so vulnerable. She fought the urge to reach out and touch his arm for comfort. Violet rounded her shoulders instead. Boone needed the truth.

"Well, you did." Violet leaned against Hawken's door. Her horse's breath came hot against her back but she stayed there. "So now you need to make that better."

Boone lifted his eyes to meet hers. "Wow. You don't hold back at all, do you?"

"Not when a little girl's heart is on the line." Violet hugged her stomach, but refused to look away.

She would make no apology for how she was speaking to Boone. The ugly scar of abandonment was too much a piece of her life story for her to overlook what he had done.

When her parents had died, she wished someone would have been brave enough to speak to her aunt and uncle this way instead of letting them shirk their duty. Allowing them to turn a blind eye to the fact that their refusal to take her meant she would spend the remainder of her childhood as a ward of the state.

No adult had fought for her.

At Hailey's age, Violet had been forced to grieve and come to terms with the loss of both her parents on her own. She wasn't okay with that happening to Hailey when she had a father who was fully capable of being there for her.

"I appreciate that." Boone's blue-green gaze met hers and his eye contact was so open and sincere, Violet couldn't help but thaw toward him a little. The man had just lost his wife. She couldn't imagine everything he was dealing with.

Boone continued talking. "It probably doesn't feel like it, but I really appreciate that you care so much about Hailey that you're willing to have a hard conversation like this for her benefit. That says a lot about you."

Violet let her shoulders relax. She rolled her eyes for effect—glad the tough part of the conversation was momentarily behind them. "It says I'm a big pain."

Boone was still shaky when he pressed away from the stall. "Actually, it says you have a big heart, which is entirely admirable."

Violet wasn't sure how to respond to such praise so she turned to face Hawken. She reached into his stall and he instantly placed his muzzle against her palm, snuffling for treats. His warm puffs of air rushed over her arm.

Boone surprised Violet by coming up beside her at the stall. He leaned his forearms on the edge of the door so he was inches from her. "I want to apologize for how I came off in the arena. Honestly? I don't want Hailey riding—I do believe it's too big a risk for her to take right now—but I could have handled that exchange better."

Violet had recently had the pleasure of getting to know Rhett, Wade and Shannon Jarrett as well as all their spouses, and they made up some of the best and kindest people Violet had ever met. But Boone Jarrett had remained a mystery. While Hailey had mourned, it had comforted Violet to paint the girl's father as the worst of men. Who else would abandon a six-year-old?

Even at the time she had known how ridiculous she was being. Hadn't the man been training to be a minster? Now she saw how wrong and terrible it had been to entertain her wild imaginings. Boone was kind like the rest of the Jarretts and had made mistakes like every other human on the planet.

Like she had.

Violet kept her attention on Hawken. "If we're coming clean, I could have handled the situation better, too." She scratched her horse's forehead. "You know, I understand your hesitancy when it comes to

Hailey and horses, I promise I do. They're powerful animals. But for what it's worth, horses are safer than most of the people I know."

Boone straightened to his full height and took a step back, giving her room. "You like them that much, huh?"

"What's not to like?" She angled her body a little so she could still give Hawken attention but could also meet Boone's gaze as well. "You can trust them with your secrets, they're excited to spend time with you no matter what you look like on any given day and they'll never break your heart."

"No, just your bones."

She batted her hand. "Good thing God gave us plenty of those."

Boone bowed his head slightly. Then he shoved his hands into his pockets and rocked forward. "Wade told me that Silas has to have a heart transplant."

A chill whooshed through Violet. She had known whatever Silas was facing had been a big deal—they only transported people by helicopters for very serious issues—but she never would have guessed something like a heart transplant. "I'm so sorry to hear that. Rhett and Macy have both been so wonderful to me. If there's anything I can do, please let me know."

Boone nodded. "Actually, there is something you can do." He held up a hand. "I'm going to warn you in advance, it's a big ask. Rhett and Macy will be living in Houston for the foreseeable future, which leaves jobs at the ranch that need to be done."

"So what's this big ask?" She had already been

doing much of Macy's work since the baby had been born and she had been pitching in helping Rhett at the summer camp, too.

"Help me run Red Dog Ranch and Camp Firefly." He took a step toward her. "We got off on the wrong foot but I promise I'm not a total bear to work with and if I'm being honest, I need your help. We have campers arriving tomorrow and I want Rhett and Macy to be able to focus all of their attention on Silas instead of worrying about what's happening here." He tipped his head to the side. "So what do you say? We'll probably have disagreements like we had earlier, but I'm committed to working through them if you are. That is, of course, if you're comfortable working alongside me. I understand if you're not."

It wasn't working with Boone that had her worried, but being more involved in Camp Firefly. As a child she had lived for the week during the summer when she got to come here. Each year, Camp Firefly had infused her with more faith and excitement about God. She had been led to believe He would rescue her from her circumstances. That He wanted to give her a home and a family.

But He never had.

And now Violet was getting pulled deeper and deeper into giving other foster kids the same false hope. It didn't sit right with her. The last few weeks with Rhett, she had only been putting things together for him to implement but she had been able to stay away from Camp Firefly for the most part. However, Boone wanted her actually involved in running the camp.

But after all the Jarretts had done for her could she say no? The Jarretts needed her help, and they'd been more than generous in giving her and Hawken a place to live after their injuries. She would just have to find a way to be helpful while also not contributing to misleading any of the children. Violet would figure out how to do that. She had overcome worse.

"I ride a horse for a living," Violet said by way of answering. "Next to controlling a thousand pounds of stubborn muscle, not much intimidates me. Least of all, working with you."

"Glad to hear it." Boone smiled. He had one of those smiles that was clearly hard won, but once it came out, it was a smile that made everyone who saw it grin back.

Including Violet.

She realized she was staring at him, so she dropped her eye contact only to notice huge wet spots all over the legs of his jeans. She gestured toward them and raised her eyebrows.

Boone glanced down. "Ah, that. On my way in I was hug-attacked by two very wet six-year-olds."

Violet chuckled. "They can be a handful."

"At least they're the good kind of handful," Boone joked.

Boone let her know he had to unpack his car and move his things into one of the open bunkhouses, but when he was done the two of them would need to sit down and come up with a plan since there were campers arriving tomorrow. Violet followed him out of the barn and watched him walk away, the whole time wondering what she had gotten herself into.

She hoped, to borrow Boone's words, she was about to be busy with the good kind of handful.

Then again, Violet had given up on hope a long time ago.

Chapter Two

The next day, Hailey skipped beside Violet as they headed to the mess hall to catch a quick lunch before camp operations would need to begin. Already, the high school- and college-aged summer staff who served as counselors at Camp Firefly were moving into their assigned cabins for the week. Last night, Boone and Violet had sat down in the ranch office together and she had run him through the normal daily schedule. They had also started bundling items for each of the activities for the week so that everything would be ready to go for the next few days. Violet had found Boone eager to learn but also nervous and reserved.

The scents of brisket and cornbread casserole tumbled down the hill to greet them. Cassidy always outdid herself, but Violet especially loved this meal. Thankfully, in the summer Cassidy had four college students as kitchen staff members who helped her feed everyone at the ranch. They took turns setting up the Sunday lunch meal so Cassidy didn't have to worry about whether or not she could attend church with her family. In exchange, Cassidy always gave them their Saturdays off, and she and Wade prepped all the Sunday food the evening before.

Hailey snagged Violet's hand and swung it. "Will you sit by me at lunch?"

Violet gave her tiny hand a squeeze. "Of course, squirt. Don't I always?"

"Well, my daddy will be there and you two did not like each other yesterday so I didn't know." She scrunched her button nose.

A six-year-old didn't need to hear all the details about her and Boone coming to a truce yesterday. She would see that they were fine together today so Violet just smiled and said, "It's a new day."

If Violet allowed herself to, she could easily start to believe that she had finally found a place for herself. It's what she had prayed for all those years ago when she was a camper here. Over the past few months she had been useful at Red Dog Ranch and now she was helping run major functions of the special place. But it was all a facade and she would do well to remind herself that Red Dog Ranch was not and never would be her home.

It was the place that had broken her heart and demolished her faith.

And once she could find a place for herself and Hawken and he was ready to be moved, she'd be gone.

The sun beat down on them and Violet wondered if it was just her, or if the hill up to the mess hall was somehow bigger and harder to climb this afternoon than it usually was. She felt sweat dotting her arms and forehead.

Hailey spotted Piper farther up the hill walking with her mom so she dropped Violet's hand and took off running to catch up with her cousin.

"Ouch, ditched for Piper." Boone's rich voice came from behind her, full of teasing.

Violet shrugged. "Eh, it happens."

"I'm just kidding." He fell into step beside her. "She really likes you. Talked my ear off about you last night. She's very impressed by the whole famous rodeo champion thing you've got going on."

"It does up my coolness factor a few points, doesn't it?" Violet joked.

Boone grinned. "Hailey could use a little cool in her life. Because my coolness factor is about at a zero these days." He laid his hand over his heart. "Who am I kidding, it probably always was a zero."

"Oh, it can't be that bad," Violet said.

"You know that motto, born to be wild? Well, mine would be more along the lines of born to be mild," Boone said. "Just being honest."

Mild was the last word Violet would have used to describe Boone.

Yesterday his T-shirt had been rumpled from traveling in the car all day. He had given off the air of someone who was visiting but didn't quite feel comfortable at the ranch. Today that was gone. He had boots, jeans, a fitted T-shirt and a cowboy hat, and the whole look was more appealing than he had a right to be. Violet's throat went momentarily dry. But she chided herself. Seeing a handsome cowboy wasn't exactly a novelty for someone who worked in the rodeo world. Boone Jarrett was handsome, yes, but he was no different from all the other men she had brushed shoulders with over the last few years.

Although that wasn't altogether correct. Boone possessed integrity and a moral fiber Violet hadn't recognized in many of the rodeo riders she met on the circuits. Most men wouldn't have apologized so readily after their spat—especially when she had been just as much to blame for the heated exchange. Last night Boone had said she had a big heart, but Violet had a hunch Boone's heart for others was enormous. Which only made his decision to leave Hailey alone during her grief even more perplexing.

Violet cleared her throat. "I didn't spot you at church this morning." Not that she had been looking. Okay, maybe she had been looking. She had presumed he would attend the same church in town the rest of his family belonged to. But Hailey had arrived with Wade's family and then they had headed to visit their mother, Mrs. Jarrett, who had recently been relocated to a retirement home that specialized in providing care for patients with memory issues.

But Violet had never seen Boone in the crowd. It wasn't as if he could have stayed at the ranch for church either because the chapel was only used for services during the week when campers were present.

Boone rubbed his hand over his jaw. "I, ah, I went to the cemetery instead this morning."

Violet's stomach fell. She instantly felt horrible and insensitive. She had just been thinking about how handsome he was while he had been mourning his dead wife. Boone wasn't just another handsome cowboy; he was a man who was struggling through one of the biggest blows that could happen in a person's life. Violet needed to remember that.

Boone stopped walking so she did, too. "I hadn't been there since I brought Hailey back after the funeral. It felt like it was time."

"I'm sure you miss her a lot." Violet could have kicked herself. What a stupid thing to say. Of course he missed his wife.

Boone put his hand over his mouth and looked toward the horizon. "June and I." He swallowed hard and scrubbed his hand over his face. "She was always there, you know? We'd been together our whole adult lives. We started dating when we were sophomores in high school. We were twenty and nineteen on our wedding day."

She hadn't asked anyone how old Boone was, but Violet knew Rhett was thirty-one and Wade was twenty-six, so Boone was somewhere in there. If she had to guess she would say twenty-eight or twenty-nine sounded about right. Counting back from sophomore year in high school would mean Boone and his wife had been together for roughly thirteen or fourteen years of their lives.

Violet rubbed her hands up her arms. "It has to be great to find someone you love at such a young age."

"Great until you lose them."

"I'm sorry."

"No, I'm sorry. You were being kind." He blew out a long, loud burst of air. "It's hard to explain. I just— I'm used to her being here." His voice hitched. "I'm used to having her as a part of my life. I'm not quite sure how to navigate without including her in my decisions. I don't know if any of that makes sense." Boone closed his eyes and pinched the bridge of his nose. His shoulders sagged.

Violet might have been the least qualified person to have this conversation with Boone. She had lost her parents when she was Hailey's age. After that she hadn't allowed herself to get close enough to anyone to hurt if they left her life. It's how she functioned for the sake of self-preservation. Being shuffled from foster family to foster family without any of them adopting her, she'd had no other choice. It was that or suffer through repeated heartbreaks. And she'd already experienced her heart breaking enough times in life to know that wasn't the path she would ever choose again.

Hopefully Boone was having these sorts of talks with Wade, too. With someone—anyone—other than her.

Violet lightly touched his arm. "I've never had something like that with another person, so I don't know. But I'm sure what you're feeling is normal. You loved her and you're hurting. Figuring out what your normal looks like now, that's going to take time, Boone. It's probably best to be gentle with yourself right now."

"Maybe what you have is better. Not loving some-one. Then this wouldn't be happening," Boone said.

Violet crossed her arms. "You don't mean that. If you hadn't loved June then Hailey wouldn't be here."

"You're right. Of course you're right," he said quickly. "Hey, I'm sorry for all of this. I shouldn't have—"

"You're allowed to talk about her, Boone. I hope you know that."

A sad smile touched his face and he nodded. "I appreciate you saying so. Sometimes it feels like I shouldn't and that's difficult." He steepled his hands together and pressed the tips of his fingers to his chin as he thought. "Want to help with something for Rhett? I initially hauled it up the hill to ask you that."

Relief washed through Violet at the change in topic. Helping was something she was comfortable wrapping her mind around.

Family and heartache, on the other hand…they made her run.

Boone kicked at the ground. He hadn't been en-tirely honest with Violet.

While he had gone to lay flowers on June's grave site this morning, he could have done it before or after church. His answer had been an excuse. Plain and simple.

The fact was, Boone wasn't ready to head to the church he had grown up in and see all the happy, churchgoing couples sitting together with their chil-dren. He wasn't ready to bump into June's parents yet. He wasn't ready for the sad looks from people he had known since childhood. And he certainly wasn't ready for the matchmaking grandmas that flooded the place.

Boone's wedding ceremony had taken place in that church.

It wasn't time to go back.

Maybe he never would.

He gestured for Violet to follow him back down the hill. "I don't think this should take too long. We should still be able to grab lunch before meeting with the counselors and if not, I'll shoot Cassidy a text for her to put some food to the side for us."

Violet raised her eyebrows. "What exactly are we doing?"

Boone glanced her way and couldn't help but notice how beautiful she was with her hair pulled up in a high ponytail. Violet definitely wore makeup but he could tell that even if she washed it off, he would have been just as captivated.

He stumbled a little as he took his next step.

During his marriage, as a way to respect his wife and honor his marriage, Boone had made a point of not noticing other women. He wasn't blind, but he had learned to save his attention and admiration for June and June alone. It was strange to not have to do that any longer. He would never stare at a woman or consider her appearance for too long—he just wasn't like that—but he was allowed to notice now. And that felt strange. It still felt wrong.

Yet he was definitely noticing Violet.

Boone coughed a little and forced himself to focus on the office building situated near the driveway. Since the last time Boone had been home, Rhett had installed a kennel and turn-out area alongside the office. Wade had let Boone know he would put Ryker in the first kennel today so he would be ready for pickup. Sure enough, a large black dog lolled in the grass in a patch of sunshine. Boone had to believe training a service animal took a lot of time and hard work. It was a wonder Rhett was able to fit it in, but Boone knew how much his brother loved working with dogs. When he had first inherited Red Dog Ranch, the eldest Jarrett had almost had to sacrifice the work he loved in order to save the family business. Macy must really support and champion Rhett's dreams for his brother to be able to shoulder so much.

Boone's gut twisted. Even after the pain he had been through, he still wanted that.

He was happy for his brother—for all his siblings and their healthy marriages. But it was odd to have the tables flipped. For eight years Boone had been the one married and they had all been single. Now he was the odd man out, left hoping one day he'd again have the companionship and love they all enjoyed. He knew it was a foolish, fleeting thought. Boone had found love as a teenager and now it was gone. He should be grateful for the time he had with June and that should be enough for him. It was greedy to want more and it felt as if he was being unfaithful to June's memory even to consider the idea of a future with another woman someday.

It wasn't time for these kinds of thoughts. He needed to focus on Red Dog Ranch and Hailey. He needed to figure out what life looked like as a single parent and what he was going to do after the summer—if he would complete seminary or take a longer break.

Boone focused back on the conversation. "Rhett used to train hunting dogs for a living. But after he took over Red Dog Ranch, he was able to go to California and take a course on training service dogs. Someone there read about him after Macy posted about the ranch online and offered to train him, free of charge."

A grin creeped onto Violet's face. "What you're telling me is Patrick is coming to pick Ryker up today?"

Right. Violet had been living at Red Dog Ranch the last few months so she would know all about Rhett starting to train service dogs and would have met Ryker already. They headed toward the office together and Violet reached the kennel first. Ryker greeted her with an excited series of whines.

"You finally get to go home today, handsome." She affixed a service dog vest onto his torso, then scratched behind his ear. "You're going to love being Howard's best friend, aren't you?" Violet looked up from her crouched position toward Boone. "Howard is Patrick's son. He's the one Ryker was trained for."

Boone scanned the other kennels. "Does anyone know where Kodiak is?" There was no way Rhett had taken his beloved dog with him to Houston. But

Boone hadn't seen the large brownish-red Chesapeake Bay retriever anywhere since his arrival yesterday. Rhett's dog was known to shadow his every step, so she had to be miserable with him gone.

Violet wiped her wrist across her brow. "She's at Wade's for now. Between Kodiak, Piper's cat and the goose Shannon left behind, poor Wade's running a zoo at his place anymore."

Once Boone was more settled and had a handle on running camp, he would have to sit down with Wade and help ease some of the responsibilities his little brother had taken on. Because it seemed as if Wade was handling more than he had originally divulged. Including caring for and providing a place for Hailey to stay while Boone had been gone. Actually, his daughter was still staying at Wade's place. She was settled there and it would take Boone a while to get his bunkhouse ready for her.

Two minutes later a large white van bumped down the driveway. Violet tossed her hands in the air and waved, signaling them to park close to the building. A thin man with an impressive mustache climbed out while a lift rose to assist a preteen boy in a wheelchair from the other side of the van. Patrick and Howard headed toward the office.

Patrick thrust his hand out to Boone. "You sure don't look like Rhett. He's taller." The man laughed and held his other hand higher than Boone's head.

"That he is." Boone shook the man's hand. "I'm Boone. Rhett's other brother."

"Wade did tell me Rhett wouldn't be able to make it today. He said you'd be able to explain."

Violet had bypassed them to bend down on one knee so she could welcome Howard. She had his hand cupped in both of hers and was listening intently to whatever the boy was telling her. She smiled warmly and nodded the whole time. By her expression no one would have known that her knee was shoved into the hard, white rocks that surrounded the kennel area. She encouraged Howard to pat the edge of his arm-rest, which signaled for Ryker to place his front paws on Howard's lap. The boy hugged the dog around the neck, a grin taking over his face as he did so.

Boone watched the exchange while he told Patrick what was going on with Silas. Rhett had texted Boone earlier, asking him to let the man know. Boone was certain that having to answer questions and field calls was probably already draining for Rhett and Macy. Boone had been overwhelmed by the bombardment of people reaching out to him after June's sudden death, and while he had appreciated knowing that people cared, sometimes he'd had to turn his phone off just to be able to make it through the day. Each call had been a reminder of his pain; each talk had wrung his emotions.

Patrick frowned and gasped twice while Boone relayed the facts about Silas's health condition. When Boone was done, Patrick put his hands up. "That sounds very serious. Now, I don't know if you know this but I own the three Chick-N-Mores in the area.

And my nearest location is my highest-grossing one as well."

Boone hadn't known Patrick owned Chick-N-More restaurants but he did know he would give anything for one of their breaded chicken sandwiches smothered in creamy jalapeno sauce right that moment. His stomach grumbled. Skipping breakfast and delaying lunch would do that, though.

Violet showed Howard another command for Ryker. Boone didn't believe Howard's smile could possibly get any bigger. No wonder Rhett loved doing this. Violet seemed to have a knack for it, too.

"I host a monthly Give Back night where a portion of the proceeds go to an organization or someone in need. I have an opening for the beginning of July and I'd love to dedicate that night to helping Rhett's family." Patrick glanced over at his son and a warm, loving smile lit his features. "I know what it's like to spend months living at a hotel so you can be near a hospital for your child. The expenses add up quickly. When Howard went through it, they didn't even let us go on the transplant list until we could pony up twenty percent of the cost." He whistled long and low. "And within the transplant community, I've heard heart transplants are the most expensive of all. So I'd love to help."

Patrick was correct. Boone had spoken to Rhett just that morning about the costs involved. Rhett and Macy had drained their bank accounts to get Silas placed on the transplant list. Heart transplants often ended up costing over a million dollars, so twenty percent of that hurt quite a bit.

"That would be amazing," Boone said. "I think Rhett and Macy would really appreciate it." He would run it by them before completely confirming the event, but Boone was certain they would be okay with anything people wanted to do to support them.

"Red Dog Ranch has helped so many people over the years." Patrick looked out over the pastures. "It's only right for the community to band around y'all."

Violet appeared at Boone's side. "Would you need us to do anything for the event?"

Patrick traced his fingers over his mustache. "Get the word out. Make flyers and drum up attention on social media. The more people who attend, the more proceeds are available to help with their expenses. It would also be fun if both of you came to help serve meals if you could. People always enjoy that sort of thing—makes it more personal. I'd even give you official Chick-N-More swag to wear."

Boone looked to Violet, who nodded excitedly. "It all sounds great. Let me talk to Rhett about it and I'll give you a call." Boone entered Patrick's number into his phone while Violet hugged Howard and Ryker goodbye.

A few minutes later when they trudged back up the hill, Boone's conscience kept bugging him. Despite their initial meeting, Violet seemed to be a good person and he had been evasive with her earlier. That wasn't how Boone wanted to live his life or act with people. Finally, he sighed and caught Violet's arm.

"I wasn't truthful earlier. When you asked me about church."

She narrowed her eyes a bit. "Boone, we hardly know each other. You don't owe me an explanation or an answer to any questions I ask."

"Listen." Boone rubbed his forehead. "I believe in being honest. It'll bother me if I don't come clean."

She had a faint smile, as if he amused her. Maybe he did. "Okay."

"Since June's funeral, I haven't been to church much. I feel bad not going. Guilty. But I just—I just can't yet." He was rambling and he wasn't even prone to rambling. Usually he spoke with such measured words and didn't mind silence. He normally waited to speak until he had the perfect, most impactful thing to say. But his words tripped out anyway. "I'm still a Christian and I believe in God and love Him and maybe I'm just making a bunch of excuses, but that's what's going on. That, and the church here in Stillwater is where I grew up going and June's parents are there and it's a lot, you know?"

"I completely get it." She squeezed his arm. "If it makes you feel better, I rarely get to attend church while I'm on circuit." She shrugged. "I'm in a new town every weekend and it's not as if there's a rodeo church." Violet chuckled. "But a few of the other athletes are believers and sometimes we'll meet somewhere or go for a hike together while we listen to an online sermon. Other times we just sit together over coffee on a Sunday morning and talk about what we've been reading in the Bible lately. We try to have some sort of community when we can."

She tilted her head, almost as if she was deciding whether she should say something else. "God lives here." She tapped his heart with a finger. "Not in a building." She quickly pulled her hand back from his chest and looked away. "I learned that at Camp Firefly."

Suddenly, Boone's eyes burned, but he chided the emotions away. After all, he had been training to be a minster. A little Sunday school message about God not being confined to a church building shouldn't bring tears to his eyes.

Boone cleared his throat. "Speaking of camp, I have to lead sermons all week for the campers." Boone grimaced a little. Not because he was against leading sermons—he was in the process of getting his master of divinity degree, after all—but knowing he would be leading a small church this week made him feel even guiltier for skipping out on services that morning. Though Violet was right. God didn't need Boone to enter a building to be with him, He already was.

Violet clapped her hands. "You'll figure it out. I don't have faith in many things, but I have faith in you, Boone. You Jarretts never let others down."

Her encouragement warmed him. "Will you be at chapel tonight?" He rocked forward. "You can give me a score on a one to ten scale when we're done." He winked, trying to make light of their conversation but secretly hoping she would say yes.

I have faith in you, Boone.

Violet chewed her bottom lip while she stared at the little chapel that shared the hill with the mess hall. She was taking so long to consider his question Boone almost broke in and asked her if she was okay.

Violet sighed and took her eyes off the chapel. "I can come tonight. Not the last night. The night the campers write on the white rocks." She hugged her middle and didn't meet his gaze. "I can't come to that night but this one should be fine."

Boone inched closer. "Violet? Is something wrong?"

"Not at all." She tucked her hair behind her ears and smiled. "Let's grab some food while it's still warm." And she headed up the hill, away from him.

Boone couldn't help but notice that her smile seemed forced.

Chapter Three

While a group of musically inclined staff members led the song time at the start of the evening chapel service for the campers, Violet met with one counselor from every cabin to answer questions and address any concerns they already had. There were two counselors assigned to each cabin, so one stayed with the campers while the other attended meetings.

From personal experience, she knew that many of the campers had gone through trauma of some kind in their life so she stressed to the counselors that they had a team of volunteer licensed therapists on call at all hours when camp was in session. If a child needed to work through issues that the college staff didn't feel equipped to deal with, Red Dog Ranch provided other resources and help.

"Our mission is to make sure every kid at camp this week feels heard, valued and loved." She scanned the group of nine counselors, making sure to meet each of their eyes. "Come see me if you or a camper needs anything. At any time."

A young man with bright red hair raised his hand. "Is it true you were a foster kid like one of our campers?"

Violet nodded. "I attended Camp Firefly for ten years." It was only natural for them to be curious. Many of the college staff members were students majoring in psychology, Christian ministry or outdoor education who were receiving class credit or fulfilling their internship requirements by working at the ranch with the kids over the summer. A handful of them were individuals who had grown up attending the camp, but most weren't.

The young man eyed Violet in a way that made her feel uncomfortable. His gaze started at her feet and moved up slowly. "Well, looks to me you turned out just fine." He smirked. "I mean, you are like a quasi-famous person for something with horses, aren't you?"

"The only thing you need to know about me is that this week I'm your boss." Violet stood, pulling her clipboard to her chest as she did. "Meeting's over. Make sure to sit with your campers at chapel, not with other staff members."

She brushed off her jeans and let them all file into the chapel while she waited outside.

A couple of bats flitted in and out of the light pooling from the flood lamps that hung around the camp area of the ranch. No doubt some of the many Mexican free-tailed bats that called the Texas Hill Country their home. The little creatures were known to eat excessive amounts of moths and other bugs so Violet had never minded them. Watching them arc and weave in the air helped calm her the same way staring up at a ceiling fan always had. She dragged in a breath, held it for a beat and then released it slowly.

Why had she agreed to come tonight?

For Boone. Violet swallowed hard. She had been so ready to dislike the man who had abandoned his daughter for eight weeks at the ranch. She still had a problem with him doing that, but she knew there was more to Boone than that mistake. And the sincerity in Boone's eyes when he asked if she would attend tonight... She hadn't been able to say no.

So far during the other weeks of camp that summer Violet had been able to steer clear of the chapel. Rhett hadn't required her attendance and her assistance hadn't ever been needed there.

Violet blew a wisp of hair from her eyes. *Settle down.* She was turning this into something much bigger than it was. She had stepped into plenty of churches in the last four years without adverse reactions.

But none of those places had ever broken her heart.

She rubbed her arm, wishing she had remembered to grab a zip-up before leaving her bunkhouse. It might have been summer in Texas, but sometimes it really cooled off once the sun went down.

She was about to go inside when she spotted Boone heading toward the chapel from the mess hall. He had a mug in one hand as he cut across the expanse between the two buildings.

"Hurry up," Violet called to him with a teasing lilt in her voice. "How are we supposed to start chapel without our speaker?"

His rich, warm laugh filled the evening air. "The great thing about being the speaker is they can't start the message without you." He winked as he got closer. "Besides, Drew's running through announcements and stressing the no-sneaking-out rule first. And you and I both know how much that man can talk." He jerked his chin toward the windows on the chapel doors. Drew had worked as a counselor at Camp Firefly for the last three years so this summer he had been given the position of assistant program director—which basically meant he was the face of camp to the campers and was with them running the games and events all day to free up Boone and Violet so they could handle other obligations.

Boone came up next to her and ducked slightly to look her in the eye. "How'd the meeting go?"

"Fine, but there's a counselor I think you should pull aside and have a talk with." She clung to her clipboard. "I haven't learned all their names yet, but he's the one with red hair."

"I know what cabin he's in." Boone took a sip from his mug. "What did he do?"

Violet gave him the word-for-word rundown. "And I would have written off the exchange but he was leering the whole time. It made my warning signals go off." Being in the rodeo meant she had learned to live and work in a male-dominated space. Given that, over the years she had begun to trust her gut when she got a strange or uncomfortable read on a man.

Boone worked his jaw back and forth. "I'll absolutely be talking to him tonight. No one should be treating you like that and him acting in such a bold way to someone in authority isn't a good sign. He's a role model and he should be acting like one even when the campers aren't present."

Violet let out the breath she hadn't realized she was holding. Some men would have brushed off her concerns, but she was quickly learning that Boone wasn't the average guy.

Violet shrugged. "I'm twenty-two so, I mean, I get that I'm close to their age but—"

"Wait." Boone's eyes went wide. "You're twenty-two?" He whistled long and low. "Man, I feel old." One hoarse laugh escaped from his lips. "I had a newborn when I was your age." He scrubbed his hand down the back of his neck, then he motioned toward the door. "I guess I better hobble on in," he joked. "It's about time for the message."

Violet held the door open but shooed him forward when he tried to wait for her. "I'll just be a minute."

When he was inside, she set her hand on the building's siding and took a deep breath. She couldn't have cared less that the guy had called her "quasi-famous." For Violet, her barrel racing career had never been about gaining renown. All she had wanted was someone, anyone, to tell her that they saw worth in her. She had thought she might achieve that by winning in the rodeos. That someone would take notice and care. Would say she was worth loving.

But no one ever had.

She was beginning to wonder if anyone ever would.

Boone had said by the time he was her age he had been married with a kid. He had been surrounded by love and on his way to making something of himself. What did Violet have to show for all her years on earth? Some awards in an event that 98 percent of the world didn't know or care about. Big whoop.

For twelve years in the foster care system no one had wanted Violet. Not one family she had lived with had seen something special enough about her to want to adopt her. Since aging out, Violet had spent the last four years trying to prove that every foster parent who hadn't adopted her had made a mistake.

None of it seemed to matter.

Maybe they had all been right not to want her after all.

Violet finally made it inside and found a seat in the back.

The small chapel had pews and stained glass windows. The junior high students who made up this week's campers fidgeted in their seats. A teen girl with tight, dark curls batted her eyes at an oblivious boy a few seats away.

Violet rolled one of the papers on her clipboard up and let it slowly unfurl on her lap. She did it again. Memories echoed in her mind. Three rows forward and to the left was the place where Violet had first prayed to ask Jesus to be a part of her life when she was ten. Toward the front was where she and her best friend, Bella, used to sit together. At least, they had until the summer Bella stopped attending because she had been adopted. Despite their childhood promises to remain best friends forever, Violet had never heard from Bella again. One more broken promise. Violet could measure her life in losses—know what age she had been in a memory based on when the person had exited her life. It was a sad realization.

Boone took the stage and introduced himself. "We're going to have a lot of fun this week and I'm looking forward to that. But right here, in this place—" he pointed down to indicate the chapel "—this is the most important part of camp. Because this is where we come to learn about God. He's the reason we're here—the very reason this ranch exists. So why don't we dive right in?"

Violet shifted in her seat. She didn't recall the pews being quite this uncomfortable. Then again, she was much younger back then. Zeroing her attention in on Boone, Violet felt the hint of a smile creep onto her face and a bit of her anxiety ebbed for a second. He had joked about being an old man but that couldn't have been further from the truth. Only six years separated them, and Violet always felt as if they were on equal footing when they spent time together or talked. Besides, with his impressive arms and wide shoulder span, Boone was in better shape than most of the guys her age.

Boone walked across the stage, the picture of ease. "Think with me about a time when you made something and it was really cool. It could be a batch of mouthwatering cookies, an art project you worked hard on, maybe a story you wrote or a dance you made up. Like all those amazing things you created, did you know that the Bible says that *we* are God's workmanship? That means you." He pointed into the crowd. "And you, and you, and me." He laid his hand on his chest. "Each one of us is His workmanship."

Violet rubbed her palms back and forth on her jean-clad thighs. She had a feeling she knew where he was going with his talk and didn't know if she could stay for it. In her youth, she had heard similar messages and they had proved to be wrong. Lies. At least in her life. They had only served to get her hopes flying high and when she crashed down, her beliefs had ended up in a thousand jagged pieces.

With no one in her life to put them—or her—back together.

Her trust in God was shaky at best right now and she didn't want anything to jeopardize that. Then again, she had promised Boone she would be at his message.

Boone paused at the center of the stage. "But what does workmanship mean, exactly? The Bible was originally written in another language and the word they translated workmanship from was *poiema*. Anyone want to repeat that with me?" He scanned the room as teenagers ducked in their chairs. "No takers?" He grinned.

A couple junior high students chuckled.

Boone nodded encouragingly. "It sounds strange,

I know. But it's a neat word because it's the same one we use to get our words *poem* and *poetry*. So if we replace the word *workmanship*, listen to this: you are God's poetry." Boone spread his hands to encompass the crowd. "You are His masterpiece. His work of art. Think of all the art kept in museums all over the world. We keep it there because people consider those pieces priceless. We put those art pieces in museums because the world has decided that art is valuable and beautiful. That it has worth and should be protected."

Violet's chest felt tight. She glanced toward the doors to make sure she had a clear pathway to the exit.

Boone stepped off the stage and leaned in toward the crowd. He dropped his voice to a stage whisper. "The greatest Van Gogh has *nothing* on you. You are a custom design by the greatest creator there ever was. Priceless. Wanted. Loved. And cherished. His workmanship. His poetry walking on earth."

Violet swallowed but she couldn't get past the burning sensation coating her throat. These kids were all those things, but she wasn't. No one wanted Violet Byrd. Not when she had been a lonely child. Not now when she was a championship racer. Her life, her existence, wasn't poetry. She was someone to be tolerated, not celebrated.

She had never been worthy.

Violet sucked in a rattling breath. A boy seated in front of her glanced in her direction.

Boone dropped down to sit on the steps leading up to the stage so he was eye level with the campers. "That's all great to hear, but it's certainly difficult to feel as if we're that valuable sometimes, isn't it? Things happen in our lives and people fail us. They make us feel like maybe we're not enough. Maybe we're not wanted. Maybe we're even unlovable."

A camper in front of Violet sniffled loudly and swiped at her eyes.

"But as a workmanship of God's hands you are valuable, beautiful and loved. And no person or circumstance can take that away from you. Because to the Father you are worth the Son, and to the Son you are worth His life. Let the power of that statement sink in." He took a moment to scan the room. "You are God's poetry on earth."

She couldn't listen to any more.

Violet burst from her seat, causing a few campers to glance her way. She forced a smile, hoping they would write off her exit as her going about her work.

Then she fled the building and didn't look back.

Boone charged down the hill. At this speed if the toe of his boot found a rock or a burrow, he would topple head over feet to the bottom. But he didn't care. He had noticed Violet's reaction to his sermon and it had twisted his heart. She had gone from anxious to ashen in minutes. Paired with her early hesitancy to even attend the chapel service, Boone knew the issue went deeper than she wanted to let on.

While he preached, he had started praying for Violet as well as the others in the audience. Whenever he gave a sermon, Boone always prayed that God would use his words, but this felt different. As wild as it sounded in his mind, this felt personal.

He had closed the service with a prayer and then handed the campers over to Drew before hightailing it after Violet. Still, she had gotten a good lead time on him and she might be tucked in her bunkhouse by now. If she was, he wouldn't disturb her. He would look around before that, though. Knowing how much she loved her horse, Boone checked the barn first but she wasn't in there. He went by the office next and then walked some of the property. He was about to give up when he spotted a lone figure sitting at the end of the dock.

The largest lake at Red Dog Ranch was located right behind the row of staff bunkhouses. The home Boone had been staying in was just off the shore and Violet's was a few buildings down. A docking pier stretched into the water and widened at the end. Violet dangled her feet over the edge.

The pier groaned with his footsteps but she didn't look his way. Boone came to a stop off to her side and a little back. "Is it okay if I join you?"

She motioned for him to go ahead and sit.

He took the spot next to her, but left some space between them. A few minutes passed. Boone decided he would wait awhile before saying something.

She stared blankly ahead. "They didn't want me." Her voice was thick with emotion. "When my parents died." She turned her head toward him and the tears he saw there tore at his heart. "I had family left. An aunt and an uncle. My parents named them in their will." She grimaced with the effort it took not to start crying again. "But they didn't want me."

"Violet," Boone said, his voice as quiet and calm as he could manage.

"I wasn't good enough." She scrubbed at her nose. "You know?"

"That's not true."

She looked up as she shook her head. "And then I came here and you people filled my head with these dreams and hopes." She pressed her fingertips to her head. "You people told me God loved me and wanted good for me and that I could trust Him with the deepest desires of my heart." Violet turned her stare on him and there was a hollow pain that left Boone feeling raw. "You said He cared. You had me spill my heart onto one of those rocks—put my greatest hope out there, and for what? For God to not want me either?" She swiped at her eyes. "Because that's sure what it feels like."

Boone reached for her and pulled her head protectively against his chest. She instantaneously fisted her fingers into the fabric on his sleeve and held on for what felt like dear life. He ran his hand over her hair and rocked a little, letting her cry. Letting her get it out. Just being there because so often words didn't heal the type of pain Violet had.

At the end of each week of camp they always had campers write the thing they were trusting God for on a rock and leave it at the foot of the cross near the chapel. That was what Violet must have been referring to. Whatever she had trusted God for, it clearly hadn't gone as she had hoped. Sometimes God's answer was no. Even to the heart of a child. But tonight wasn't the time to wade into that difficult discussion with her.

"One of my foster moms taught me how to barrel race," she whispered into his chest. "That's how I learned. I thought…if I won and she was proud… I thought…" Her body trembled.

Boone brushed her hair back into place. The strands kept clinging to the stubble on his jaw. "You thought they would adopt you and they didn't."

She nodded against him. "I aged out and had to leave."

"I'm so sorry, Violet," he whispered. "I'm sorry for everything."

She slipped out of his arms and hugged her middle. "I've asked myself a million times what's wrong with me. Something has to be. There has to be a reason no one wants me."

Boone fought the urge to pull her into his arms again. But he couldn't hug her pain away and he hadn't earned the right in her life to attempt such a thing, either. Nothing about him could chase away the lies she believed. Only God could do that for her.

"There's nothing wrong with you." He spoke gently. "Just like I said back there—you are a priceless masterpiece and God—"

She shot to her feet. "It's so easy for you to spew that stuff, isn't it? It's easy to talk about being loved and wanted when you have never felt devalued or unworthy a day of your life."

Taken aback by the swift change in her tone, Boone was slow to rise to his feet. "Violet."

"You're telling them lies, Boone." She flung an arm in the direction of the chapel. "Don't you get that? You're causing foster kids further pain by spooning a bunch of sugary ideas their way. You shove dreams into their heads and promise they'll come true and aren't there to deal with the fallout when those dreams never happen."

Boone held up his hands in surrender. "That's not fair."

"Know what's not fair?" Violet whirled to face him again. "You have a family that has always loved you, always supported you, always wanted you. You have no idea what this feels like." She jabbed a finger at him. "You have a daughter out there who adores you and you still haven't moved her to your bunkhouse—you're still not the one taking care of her. *That's* what's not fair. So don't preach your platitudes to me, minister. Because I don't want them."

Violet sidestepped his outstretched hand and didn't look back any of the times he called her name.

Chapter Four

Violet was on her way to the office when Hailey bounded out of the bunkhouse situated closest to the lake. She brought her hand up to shield her eyes from the onslaught of the afternoon sun as she called out a greeting to the little girl.

After spending the morning doing physical therapy on both herself and Hawken, Violet had stopped back at the staff house assigned to her so she could clean up and change before heading to the office for the rest of the day. Not that she would admit to it, but she had spent a few extra minutes in front of the mirror, anxious over the prospect of seeing Boone again. She had been able to avoid encountering him in person for a few days as he got settled, and then he and Hailey had traveled to Houston to visit Rhett and Macy and meet Silas. He had kept up with Violet about the ranch and helped make decisions regarding Camp Firefly over the phone, but Wade had let her know Boone would be back in the office today.

She wanted to be sure she looked confident and poised—much different from the mess he had held in his arms and tried to comfort a few nights ago. Falling apart in front of Boone...that hadn't been her style. She needed to get back on track.

The cowboys on the rodeo circuit had nicknamed her the Vault because she never shared, never hinted at what was going on in her head and never let it show when her contenders got the best of her. They had respected her and considered her a strong woman because of it.

The Vault. Violet snorted. If those cowboys could see her now.

So far, she had behaved more like a colander. At least around Boone. Ever since she had discovered that he left Hailey at the ranch for eight weeks, the memories of being abandoned at the same age had come back to bite at the veneer of self-assurance she had long ago learned to wear. And the emotions associated with remembering were leaving her raw. However, it would do no one—least of all her—any good to pull her hurt out only to turn it over and over in her hand like a broken trinket. It was time to be an adult and pack all her baggage away.

Boone was back. It was a fresh start.

She would be the Vault once more.

Hailey hop-danced into Violet's path, the girl's long honey-blond hair swaying with each movement. "Want to hear something cool? You'll never guess. Want to hear it?"

Violet stopped and bent to meet the little girl's

eyes. "Do I want to hear about it? Are you kidding me, squirt?" She would always stop whatever she was doing to be interested in what mattered to Hailey because she knew how much that would have meant to her at that age. "Of course I want to hear whatever you're excited about."

"I got to move in with Daddy," Hailey said. "Last night when we got home, he moved the rest of my stuff here from Uncle Wade's house."

Violet glanced toward the bunkhouse. Had Boone already been planning on moving Hailey or had her harsh words the other night prompted his actions? Not that it mattered. All that mattered was that Hailey was with her dad again. Where she belonged. Violet hoped they had been able to bond a lot on their trip to see Silas.

"How do you feel about leaving Wade's house?"

"Really good. I love my dad." Hailey bobbed her head. "It's a tiny bit sad not to be in Piper's room with her." She held up her fingers showing an inch of space between her thumb and pointer finger. "But my dad said I could still do sleepovers with her and maybe she could come stay in my new room soon. And he said Uncle Rhett won't mind at all if we paint the walls. I'm thinking purple or teal or maybe something else. Dad said I can choose for my room."

"Sounds like that could be a lot of fun."

Hailey grinned. "I think so. Hey, and you could sleep over, too!"

Footsteps crunched on the ground behind them.

"Who's sleeping over?" Boone's voice. Of course this would be when he arrived.

Slowly, Violet rose to stand again. The laugh that escaped her lips had an undercurrent of nerves she hoped Boone didn't pick up on. She kept her gaze on Hailey. "How about we plan a sleepover where you and Piper come to *my* house instead. It can be a girls-only party."

Hailey grabbed Violet's hand and pumped it as she jumped up and down. "Oh! Can we really?"

"As long as it's fine with your dad and Piper's parents." Violet pivoted to finally bring Boone into their conversation.

Boone's expression was soft as he studied her face. "I'm sure we could make that work." He turned and pulled Hailey into a hug. "But I get you to myself for a little bit first before we start planning nights away, okay?"

Hailey's thin arms came around her dad's neck. Boone's daughter pressed her mouth close to his ear and whispered something. The sight caused sadness to prick Violet's eyes. She was happy Hailey finally had her dad's attention, but it also reminded Violet of all she had missed out on in her life and everything she would never have.

Get a hold of yourself.

Hadn't she just decided she was going to be cool and professional around Boone? The fact that the man could hurdle over her defenses without even knowing he was doing so irrationally irritated her.

Violet took a few steps away. "All right, well, I'm going to head down to the office."

Boone cleared his throat. "Wait up." He lifted Hailey into his arms and his large stride ate up the distance between them in seconds. "Hailey has a question for you."

"Since we can't do our girls party yet we want to invite you to dinner tonight. It's at our house. Will you come?"

Violet raised an eyebrow in Boone's direction.

Boone grinned. "Yes, *we* are inviting you over. I figured you and I need some time to brainstorm for the event for Silas at Chick-N-More anyway—at the office we'll be pulled in a million directions with everything at the ranch and camp. Unless you don't want to plan in your off-hours—I completely understand that, too."

"I don't mind at all." Violet wanted to ask about Silas but it would probably be better to wait until Hailey wasn't around and Boone could speak candidly. "I think dinner's a great idea."

"Great idea, huh?" He winked at his daughter. "She must not know about my cooking yet."

Hailey giggled. "He's the worst!" She stuck out her tongue and grabbed at her throat as if the idea of eating food her dad prepared would make her sick.

Boone wrinkled his nose. "I'm not *that* bad."

"He is." Hailey nodded. "He burns oatmeal."

"In his defense, oatmeal can be tricky," Violet offered.

Boone's hand shot into the air, ready for Violet to

give him a high five. Not one to leave someone hanging, Violet complied. Boone hooted like a sports fan who had just watched the ending to a close championship game. "See, at least someone around here is on Team Dad."

Violet thought back to the night she had left the chapel service and had accused him of feeding the campers false hope. She had wondered if their interactions would be awkward or stilted when they saw each other again but Boone wasn't acting as if he was offended by what she had said. Perhaps he was being normal for Hailey's sake, but Violet didn't think so. Boone was nothing if not genuine and sincere in his interactions. She still wanted to apologize for how she had stormed off on him so they could put it in the past, but now wasn't the time for that, either.

He spun Hailey around in a circle and then smiled over at Violet. "I'll be in the office in about a half an hour. Have to drop the rug rat off at her grandparents' house for a visit first."

Given the fact that Boone's father had passed away last year and his mother lived in a memory care facility, he had to be talking about June's parents. Violet had momentarily forgotten that they lived in town—that June would always be a very present part of Boone's life. For a second Violet had felt as if...

So foolish. A few smiles and kind words from a nice guy and Violet had lost the good sense that had protected her in the romance department for so many years. Like the rest of the Jarretts, Boone was simply kind and was making sure she felt welcome and included. They all acted this kindly at Red Dog Ranch. Reading anything else into his actions would do Violet no good. Besides, she didn't want anyone flirting with her. She wouldn't know the first thing about being in a relationship, which was why she avoided them.

She forced all thoughts about Boone from her mind. Not an easy task with the man standing nearby.

Hailey cupped her hands to her dad's cheeks. "I am not a rat! I'm a rug mouse, remember? A cute little mouse." Hailey held up her hands to be little paws and squeaked a few times.

Boone slung her over his shoulder. "How could I forget?" He tipped his chin to Violet and then headed toward his car with his daughter giggling as he carried her away.

From her booster seat in the back, Hailey kicked the passenger seat. Boone used the rearview mirror to check on her. Her brow was scrunched and her lips were pursed. On their trip to Houston, Hailey had asked a lot of hard questions and had wanted to talk about June a lot. The conversations had gutted Boone and he wasn't sure he could keep having them without falling apart. He had been trying so hard to be strong and put on a brave face so his daughter wouldn't worry. Because Boone knew if he allowed himself to sink a toe into his grief it wouldn't be long until a riptide of emotions would drown him completely, which wouldn't do Hailey any good.

He glanced in the mirror again, catching her eyes.

She looked so much like June it made his chest feel too tight to take a decent breath. "What are you thinking about, sweetheart?"

She stopped tapping her foot. "I like Violet a lot."

Boone offered a soft smile. "You've mentioned that a time or two."

"No, like, I wish she had come with us right now." Hailey looked out the window as she hugged her stomach. "I think it would have made me feel a little better."

His gut clenched. Sometimes going to June's parents' house made Hailey sad. While she loved spending time with her grandparents and they were great people, it was a huge reminder of what Boone and Hailey had lost. Photos of June graced every room and June had been the spitting image of her mother. It was difficult for Boone to see them, too, so he understood any inner turmoil Hailey might be feeling, but it was important for his daughter to have a strong relationship with June's family. That would have mattered to June, so it mattered to him. But his late wife's parents owned an RV and spent a large portion of the year traveling around the country so he needed to make use of the time they were in town.

"Your grandparents love you a lot, you know that, right? You don't need to be afraid, but if you want me to stay with you while you're there, I can." Boone had been away from the ranch for a few days so he knew that despite Wade, Drew and Violet handling issues, there was still work waiting for him in the office. At the hospital, Rhett had given him specific instructions about a list of things to take care of that the others wouldn't know about. But Hailey's well-being was important to Boone and he was beginning to realize how much he had failed her by going back to Maine after June's funeral.

While dealing with his responsibilities at school had been the logical choice…maybe it hadn't been the *best* choice.

Hailey sighed. "You're not listening."

"What are you trying to tell me?"

"When you weren't here, Violet helped me miss Mommy less. She makes me happier when she's around. She understands." Hailey scratched her nose. "Do you think that's okay with Mommy?" Her little voice hitched. "Would Mommy be mad that I like hanging out with someone else?"

Boone grasped the steering wheel tighter. He swallowed, once, twice. Cleared his throat. "No, baby, she wouldn't be mad. Mommy would love anything that made you happy. She loved you so much and would want whatever's best for you." The last words came out quiet. His throat burned with the weight of them and he couldn't say anything more.

"Do you think Mommy would have liked Violet?"

Boone considered her question. While Violet and June shared a few similarities—they were both about the same height and had the same straight blond hair—there was so much about them that was different, too. For most of her life June had been quiet and careful, which was what had made her and Boone such a great match. She had been content to read a book in a nearby chair while he was studying. She had been fine to stay inside weekend after weekend and binge-watch shows while he worked on sermons. She would wake up before him and they would talk about deep topics over breakfast and they shared a peaceful sort of love that had seemed to suit them well. Their life together hadn't been exciting or adventurous, but it had been theirs and that had been enough.

While Violet certainly didn't strike Boone as someone who wanted to be at a party every day, she was used to a more fast-paced and exciting lifestyle. The rodeo wasn't a career for the faint of heart. She had to move constantly and ride in a daring way over and over again to keep her ranking in the circuit. As long as she was a barrel racer, she would need to travel. Boone couldn't picture Violet happy at home without much to do or content to quietly exist around another person. Not the woman who had gone toe to toe with him the first time they had met.

Then again, after three miscarriages and failed attempts at fertility treatments, June had started to take more risks, too. For a while there, they almost separated. A fact Boone had never shared with anyone. When June announced she had signed up to go on a weeklong hiking trip with some of the other ladies at their church, Boone had been excited for her. He had prayed it would be a life-changing time.

June had died on that trip.

Boone turned up a tree-lined road that marked the residential area where his late wife had grown up. "You know, I think they would have liked each other a lot." Boone thought back to the other night on the pier with Violet.

They didn't want me.

There has to be a reason no one wants me.

Boone hadn't known what to say to help her, but June would have. His wife had seemed to possess a radar that helped her identify hurting women. She had always known how to encourage them and over the years she had taken many of the college-aged women at their church under her wing.

"Your mom would have been fascinated with Violet's barrel racing career and would have enjoyed talking to her." Boone let out a shaky breath. "And she certainly would have loved how much Violet seems to care about you."

He pulled into his in-laws' driveway and shifted the car into Park.

"Violet's all alone," Hailey said. "Just like us."

Boone swung around in his seat so he could face his daughter while they talked. "We're not alone, sweetheart. We're surrounded by my family and your mom's parents and—"

"We're not…it's not the same anymore. It feels like a different kind of alone." She unbuckled her seat belt and opened the door. Hailey looked back at him. "I'm glad Violet's coming for dinner. Even if you ruin the food."

June's mother waved at them from the front doorway. When Boone had set up this visit for his daughter, he had told his in-laws that it would be a quick drop-off so he could head back to the ranch.

He caught Hailey's arm before she could leave the car. "I love you, Hailey. I love you so much. You and me—we're a family. It's a small family, but it's my favorite one."

She looked down. "I know. But I liked three better than two."

"Me, too, sweetheart." His voice was raw.

She slipped out of his hold and jogged up the driveway, diving into her grandma's arms. June's mom waved to Boone again before closing the door.

Boone forced himself to stay numb as he navigated his car out of the driveway and around the block. Far enough so he knew he was out of sight from the house before he pulled over, tossed the gearshift back into Park and pressed his forehead into the steering wheel.

"Why did You take her?" His voice came out as weary as his faith felt in that moment. "Where are You in this?"

You people told me God loved me and wanted good for me and that I could trust Him.

Violet had been right to lash out at him. How many times had he attempted to encourage someone with those exact words? Perhaps he was a fraud because he wasn't even certain he still believed them. After a year when he had lost his dad, his mother had been diagnosed with early-onset Alzheimer's, his sister had been trapped in an abusive relationship, his brother had battled cancer, Boone had lost his wife and now his tiny nephew needed another baby to die in order to live—could he still trust God?

For the first time in his life, Boone didn't know how to answer that question.

Then he lost it—lost himself in a way he hadn't since first receiving the call about June's death. His shoulders and chest quaked with his loud sobs. His arms ached from gripping the steering wheel so tightly. He called out to God. Asked the same questions again and again.

But he found no answers.

Chapter Five

Violet cradled the small pan of s'mores bars she had made to take along to Boone's house for dinner. Hopefully she wasn't stepping on any toes by bringing dessert. If they didn't want the treats, she would take them back to her place. She'd been known to polish off a pan on her own in two or three days. Or less.

Earlier in the afternoon, Boone had sent a text letting her know he would probably miss her at the office because he had to head to the large ranch house that belonged to Rhett and Macy to take care of some things for his eldest brother. Rhett had an office in the house that had been neglected since he had been gone. Because of that, she still hadn't been able to talk to Boone about her breakdown the other night. Now she was questioning if she should bring it up at all. Perhaps it was better to act as if that evening hadn't happened.

If he didn't mention it then she wouldn't, either.

She clutched her pan a little tighter and lifted her chin.

Violet wanted to hear how Silas was doing. She was there to see Hailey and to pitch in with brainstorming for the fundraiser for Silas. Not to make nice with Boone Jarrett.

No matter how much she wanted to.

The Vault didn't talk about personal things with anyone—least of all a handsome man with a kind smile who possessed the ability to give the safest, most perfect hugs. Whose hand cupping the back of her head, whose heartbeat under her ear, felt like a welcome—a home—she had never known before.

Violet let out a loud puff of air. Thoughts like that stopped now.

As she was coming up the walk that led to Boone's bunkhouse the front door swung open. Hailey's tiny frame appeared in the doorway and she started waving a red dish towel as if she were a matador and Violet were the bull.

"Dad burned the garlic bread," she called. "It was bad. The alarm went off and everything." She waved her towel wildly back and forth, apparently ushering smoke out of the small house. Boone materialized behind her and gave an exaggerated shrug before snatching the dish towel from Hailey's hands.

He tossed the towel onto his shoulder. "So, the good news is the smoke seems to be mostly out of here. Bad news is the bread is definitely not salvageable."

"It's hard. Like a brick," Hailey said.

A pungent odor of burnt bread wafted to where Violet stood and she coughed a little.

One of Boone's eyebrows rose.

Violet laughed. "I'm sorry. I'm not laughing at you. I'm really not."

The hint of a smile tugged at Boone's lips as he shook his head. "Man, invite a pretty lady over and the first thing she does is laugh at me. See if I do that again." He eased the pan from her hands. "Well, this looks better than anything I made."

Hailey latched onto Violet's hand and dragged her into the house. The smoke smell was much stronger inside but all the windows were open and multiple fans were running. They had done everything they could to remedy the odor.

Violet nodded toward the pan as Boone set it on the table. "It's so easy to make. You take premade cookie dough and mix in a little less than a cup of crumbled graham crackers and bake that. Once it's done you spread some marshmallow cream on top and then sprinkle that with another half cup of crumbled graham crackers and bake it a little longer and presto, done."

"Sounds delicious," Boone said.

Hailey licked her lips. "I feel like I could eat ten of those."

Boone tilted his head. "It still smells like smoke in here, doesn't it?"

Violet batted her hand. "The fans are helping. It'll be gone shortly."

Boone rubbed his neck and sighed. Stress was evident in the set of his shoulders. Violet's heart squeezed. He was trying—trying to make a nice night because his daughter had asked him to—and that was really touching.

Violet laid a hand on his arm. "It's not a big deal. We've all been there."

"I'm not—" Boone sighed. "I'm not very good at this kind of thing. My wife..." His voice trailed off.

Violet squeezed his arm. "I know." She kept her voice soft. "Starting over. Learning new things at our age is rough. And we're not even that old." She let her hand drop away. "I've only known riding since I was a teen and now I'm having to navigate so many new things. I don't always succeed, either."

He leaned closer. "I've yet to see you fail at anything you try."

Hailey banged plates onto the table. "It's all ready."

As they took their seats, Violet's stomach felt as if she had swallowed an army of ants. And she knew the sensation had nothing to do with being hungry. The things Boone said, the sincerity in his eyes when he looked at her—it was impossible not to be affected.

On the table there were some really thick cuts of chicken covered with cream sauce in a pan and what looked like a bowl of instant mashed potatoes. Some people might have turned up their nose at the meal and lack of vegetables but Violet didn't mind. She was used to eating whatever was available when she was on the road. The gesture of someone making dinner was enough for her—the menu didn't matter. It was just nice to actually be invited to share someone's table for once.

Boone ladled food onto three plates. Then he

reached out his hands, taking one of Hailey's and one of Violet's, before bowing his head. Hailey's hand snaked over and took Violet's other one, completing their little circle around the table.

"Thank You, God, for this day, for a home to stay in and meaningful work here at the ranch. Be with Rhett and Macy and baby Silas. Help sustain Silas as he waits for a heart. Thank You for sending Violet to the ranch—she has been a blessing in Hailey's life and we're thankful to be able to share a meal with her. In Jesus's name." Everyone whispered *amen* as Boone ended the prayer.

Warmth flooded Violet's chest as she released both of their hands. She wanted to drink in the moment so she could remember it forever. Because here, for a span of time this evening, she was wanted.

It wasn't something Violet had experienced very often in her life.

"Hey, Dad. I was thinking." Hailey picked up a fork and bounced in her seat. "Can I start doing riding lessons with Violet again?"

"I… Let's table that subject for now." Boone avoided making eye contact with Violet.

"But, Dad—"

Boone lowered his chin. "Hailey, it's not safe. Okay? It's not something I'm comfortable with you doing."

So much for feeling wanted. Violet ran her fork through her mashed potatoes. If Violet could have sunk any further into her chair, she would have.

Hailey flung her hand toward Violet. "But Violet does it and she's fine."

Boone's eyes darted to Violet's.

Violet pushed her palms against the table and sucked in a fortifying breath. "I did get hurt riding a few months ago so your dad's concerns are very real. I love horses and I trust Hawken, but even with that, accidents happen and horses are very big. I see where your dad is coming from." She wanted to say that anything could be dangerous though and with practice, horses were worth the risk. But she didn't. Now wasn't the time.

Hailey crossed her arms over her chest.

Boone mouthed *thank you*.

"I can't wait to eat." Violet was willing to do anything to change the subject. She grabbed her fork again and scooped a huge bite of mashed potatoes into her mouth. Instantly her eyes started watering and despite her best effort to not make a scene, she gagged. Loudly.

Boone frantically pressed a cup of water into her hands. Violet took it and snatched her napkin in the other. She turned slightly, spitting the mashed potatoes into it before downing the water. She coughed. Her eyes felt as if they were on fire as she wheezed a few more times. "How much salt did you put in those?"

Boone stared at her wide-eyed. "Whatever was on the box. A fourth of a cup. I think?"

Violet got up and fished the box from where it rested near the oven. She coughed again as she scanned the instructions. "Oh, Boone." Violet groaned. "It calls for a fourth of a teaspoon."

Hailey slid her plate toward Boone. "The chicken is still all pink."

Boone sliced his piece of chicken in half and then grabbed Violet's plate and cut into that chicken, too. "None of it is cooked all the way." He sighed and started gathering up the plates. He carried everything over to the trash can and started scraping the plates.

Violet caught his arm. "Hey, it's okay."

"If I reheat the sauce it'll break. It's made with heavy cream. I know that much about cooking." He stepped away and dropped the plates into the sink. He pointed at the pan of s'mores bars but his smile was clearly forced. "I guess it's dessert for dinner, then?"

Hailey let out a whoop behind them.

"Not so fast." Violet pulled open the fridge to scan the contents. She prayed for something to salvage the night.

"There's not much there." Boone came up behind her.

Her gaze landed on a package of hot dogs. If she remembered correctly, there was a firepit not far behind Boone's bunkhouse near the lake that was sometimes used for camp programs. She grabbed the hot dogs and spun around, bringing her inches away from Boone's broad chest. She sucked in a sharp breath. "Can you build a fire?"

Hailey hummed the first few notes of "Do You Want to Build a Snowman." Then burst out with, "Do you want to build a fire?" She started skipping around the small kitchen island while she continued making up lyrics. "Or roast some hot dogs outside? My daddy burned the dinner. But it's okay. 'Cause Violet made it better. Do you want to build a fire?"

In complete dad mode, Boone nodded and continued his conversation with Violet as if Hailey wasn't dancing around them belting out a song. "Now that, I can do."

"It doesn't have to be a big fire," Hailey sang.

"Go start that." Violet pointed at him. She snagged Hailey on her next trip around the island. "Hailey and I will go hunting for some good sticks."

Boone was out the door a minute later. Hailey helped Violet clean up the kitchen and put away everything Boone had used to make their dinner and then they cut up some watermelon, found some paper plates and carried everything outside. By the time they reached the firepit, Boone had a strong fire going. Hailey found a few long branches and Boone and Hailey roasted hog dogs while Violet divvied up watermelon, buns and s'mores bars onto everyone's plates.

After eating, they ended up staying outside for the rest of the evening. Rhett's dog, Kodiak, wandered to the lake and Hailey tossed balls and branches into the water over and over again for the dog. Kodiak never seemed to tire.

Violet used her hand to shield her eyes from the bright sunset. "Your brother trained that dog how to do water rescues. It's pretty amazing to watch."

Boone stood shoulder to shoulder with Violet as

they looked over the lake. "I don't doubt it. My big brother has always been a bit of a hero who can accomplish anything he puts his mind to. I've always looked up to him." Boone heaved a sigh. "I've been meaning to tell you, you were right." He gestured toward where his daughter played with the big dog. "I should have moved her back to my house right away. I honestly don't know why I didn't."

Even though there was no way Hailey could overhear them, Violet dropped her voice. "Because you were scared, Boone. You were afraid you wouldn't know how to manage her on your own—especially with all you two have been through. You thought she'd be safer somewhere she couldn't see you ever be sad or worried." He opened his mouth to say something, but she plowed on before he could. "But being scared is okay. People think it's not, but it is. That little girl would rather have her dad nearby and terrified about the future than not have him around at all." Violet finally met his gaze. "She doesn't need a perfect dad, just a present one."

Boone excused himself soon after in order to put Hailey to sleep. Hailey gave Violet a huge hug before she headed inside.

"I love you," Hailey whispered, her sticky hands winding around Violet's neck.

Violet hugged her close. "You too, squirt."

Once she was alone, Violet wrapped her arms across her middle and watched the sun sink below the horizon. When it was finally gone, she headed over to the campfire and started gathering everything.

Kodiak padded after her and sprawled out a few feet from the firepit. Violet couldn't help the smile that came to her face as she thought about the evening and how much fun it had been to spend time with Boone and Hailey. Even the hard conversation she and Boone had shared had gone well.

It had felt how she had always imagined home would feel. A family. People who laughed and made the best of a bad situation and who helped one another. People who simply enjoyed being together.

Violet froze as she was setting the last cup on the tray.

Boone and Hailey weren't her family.

Her fingers tightened around the cup. Kodiak lifted her head and let out one low whine.

She couldn't think like that.

Violet set down the last cup with more force than necessary.

She refused to let herself feel at home. Not here, not anywhere. Doing so only ever ended in rejection and heartbreak.

With two mugs in his hands, Boone stepped outside only to see Violet heading out of the yard. She was running off, just like she had the night on the pier. He hadn't brought up that night because so much time had passed, and it seemed as if she didn't want to talk about it.

Maybe he should let her sneak off without a goodbye. She didn't owe him any niceties. But he was so tired of being alone every night after he put Hailey to bed. Sick of the quiet. Of being stuck with only his thoughts. Maybe he was being selfish, but Boone wanted Violet's company even if it was only for a few more minutes.

"Wait up," he called after her. When she pivoted in his direction he said, "I made hot chocolate."

She had her hands on her hips and stood on the edge of the yard for a few more minutes. Her shoulders were set into a hard line. In the dim evening light her outline appeared so small, so fragile. Boone's chest suddenly ached with a desire to protect her, but he shook that thought away just as quickly. Violet was a strong, capable woman who had gotten along just fine before they met. She didn't need or want anything Boone had to offer.

Not that he was in the market to offer everything anyway.

He strode in her direction, holding one of the mugs out. "If there's one thing I can make without ruining, it's hot chocolate." He took a step closer. "It's opening packages and boiling water. Pretty high-palate stuff here—you don't want to miss out."

She edged forward and lifted the cup from his hand. "I happen to love hot cocoa."

He jerked his head in the direction of the firepit and she nodded. They slowly picked their way across the yard back toward the seating area near the fire.

Violet squinted into her mug. "Are those…? You put Lucky Charms marshmallows in here?" Her shoulders finally eased. Her green eyes darted to meet his.

Boone bumped her shoulder as they sat down. "That's my specialty." He winked. He took a sip.

"Hailey actually hates the marshmallows in her cereal but loves the other part of it. Weird, I know. Usually it's the other way around." He shook his head. "So we pick them out and put them in a baggie to use in other stuff—namely hot chocolate. Now you know all our family secrets."

Violet cupped her hands around her mug. She gazed toward the fire for such a long time, he almost asked her if something was wrong. But then she swallowed and slowly turned to meet his eyes. "I was wrong about you. You're a good dad, Boone."

Her words made his eyes burn. He wasn't a good dad. He had abandoned his daughter in her grief. Since June's death he had made so many mistakes. His throat felt raw and it had nothing to do with the temperature of his hot chocolate.

He stared into his mug as he swirled the liquid around, watching the marshmallows smear colors like an oil slick over the top of his drink as they melted. "I'm not so sure about that. Since June… I'm failing at everything I do."

It had taken a week of thinking, but Boone had finally pinpointed why he had returned to school instead of staying at the ranch with Hailey and the rest of his family. Sure, he had gone to close down their life in Maine, but there had been more to it. School and studying had always come easily to Boone. Out of all the Jarretts, he was the book-smart one, the reader, the test-acer. He had gone back to school because it was the only thing he felt successful at. He hadn't wanted to face how he was failing Hailey by not knowing how to walk through grief. He hadn't wanted to struggle in front of siblings who had always looked to him for advice, and he hadn't wanted to face how he'd failed June, too. Because their marriage had been built around pursuing his dreams. His plan.

Had he ever even stopped to ask what her dreams were?

Now it was too late.

"Boone, no." Violet set her mug on the seat beside her so she could place a hand on his knee. "Thinking like that won't get you anywhere."

He tried to swallow. "I don't know how to do this. All this, without her. I miss her so much and I feel like I'm fumbling everything with Hailey. And I don't know what to do about it."

Violet never took her eyes from his face. "Okay, so you can't take back the eight weeks you were gone, but you can do and have been doing everything in your power to be there for Hailey since then." She jiggled his knee a little. "And that's all she needs, Boone. She just needs you."

He set down his mug so he could run a hand over his close-cropped hair. "She wanted to have a nice dinner and look how that turned out."

Violet gestured toward the firepit area. "Think about the memory she made today. She'll remember having an impromptu campfire dinner and playing with Kodiak and making up songs. She'll remember how cool it was that her dad let her stay up late."

He set his hand on top of hers. "What she'll remember most is how her friend Violet swooped in and saved the day." His fingers instinctively curled around hers. "You're the real MVP here."

Violet slipped her hand free. She rubbed both her arms. "I'm sorry about your wife. I don't think I've said that yet."

Kodiak got up and ambled to lie down next to his feet. She let out a loud harrumph.

"Thank you." Boone hunched over, his elbows on his knees. "We'd been together since we were kids. A life with June is all I've ever known." He knew he was rambling, but Boone couldn't stop. He hadn't been able to verbalize these things to anyone else. "And Hailey is going to slowly lose her—I already see it beginning. Will she remember her mom when she's fifteen? I don't know. She's so young and June's going to miss so much."

"I lost both my parents in a car accident when I was her age. I walked away with a couple bumps and they both were gone before the police arrived on scene." She pulled the zip-up hoodie she was wearing tighter around herself. "But I remember them. I can still recall the smell of my mother's perfume and her voice—it was always calm, never flustered. And my dad, he loved to watch *Jeopardy* and those chocolate oranges were his favorite candy. I won't ever lose those things about them." She sighed as if telling him those details had cost her something. "You can't bring June back, but you can honor her memory and her love for you guys. You can help Hailey see that she's a piece of everything you both do—when you guys have fun or when either one of you is sad, and she's a part of how you guys love and are there for each other."

She leaned her shoulder into his. "Don't get so wrapped up in what's going wrong that you don't see what's right. Don't let Hailey lose the dad she's always known by turning inward or focusing on mistakes. Just be there, be present. That's what she needs."

"I'm sorry you went through this when you were a child. No one should have to."

Violet shrugged but it seemed forced. "Death is the price for life, right? Anyway, it was a long time ago." She dusted off her jeans and stood, striding a few feet closer to the fire so her back was to him. The woman in front of him had been through so much pain in her lifetime yet she was kind and encouraging. He fought the urge to get up and wrap his arms around her from behind.

"Violet—"

She spoke over him. "You're talking to your siblings about all these things, right?"

Boone scrubbed his hand over his head. "I haven't, actually. Rhett needs to focus on Macy and Silas, Wade has plenty on his shoulders as it is, and with her travels Shannon is almost impossible to reach. I don't want to burden any of them." He stood, too, and made his way to her side. He shoved his hands into his pockets to keep from reaching out to her. "Besides, I've always been the one they come to for advice. That's been my role in our sibling group." And he didn't want them to think he was incapable. He was supposed to end up being a pastor, after all. No one wanted a pastor who wasn't able to keep their life together. It was good training for him to deal with this on his own.

Violet's smile was sad. "Listen, maybe it's not my place. After all, I don't have much experience with family or love for that matter, but I have to imagine that people who love you aren't ever going to see you or your struggles as a burden." She stepped out of the ring of light cast by the fire. "You should start talking to them, Boone. You have people in your life—you don't know how rare that is. Don't take them for granted."

She said good-night and headed back to her bunkhouse. But Boone stayed near the fire waiting for it to peter out so he could make sure it was completely extinguished before he went to bed. Kodiak stayed beside him. Boone shot Wade a quick text, letting him know he would keep the dog at his place for the night. He should probably take over her care completely until Rhett came home. Having Kodiak's company was better than being alone.

Violet's words played through his mind. For someone who claimed not to know anything about love, her advice was covered in it. She spoke truth but worded it gracefully. She knew how to challenge in an encouraging way. She spoke with love and all her actions with Hailey showed how much love was waiting in Violet's heart.

She just needs you.

After their conversation, Boone couldn't help but wonder what it would be like for Violet to need him, too.

Chapter Six

The next morning Violet woke earlier than usual and decided to make good use of her time instead of staying in bed. Only months ago, she would have saddled Hawken and they would have explored new trails together, but Hawken couldn't handle a rider yet.

Please, let him heal.

She headed to the barn and hooked a lead line to his halter, and they started off on a slow walk side by side across the fields of Red Dog Ranch. She could have worked him in the large, newly built riding arena located just behind the barn, but Hawken had spent so much time inside stalls lately that Violet made sure to bring him outside every chance she could. Even though it was early, it was already hot, so she decided not to push her horse too far. He needed to be exercised daily but it was important to not overdo it.

When her parents died, their assets had been placed into a fund Violet was only able to access once she turned eighteen. After aging out of the system and leaving the Jenningses—the foster family who had taught her to barrel race—she had tapped into her parents' money to purchase Hawken. He had already been trained on the barrels but the girl who originally owned him had left him in a stall at a rental facility when she went to college. Unridden and unwanted for months, Hawken had developed an attitude and had started biting the helpers at the barn. His owner had decided to offload him for a song.

Violet trailed her fingers down his neck, causing him to nicker softly.

The first time she met him, Violet knew Hawken was the one. Abandoned and angry—they had understood each other all too well. They had both had something to prove. In the beginning, Violet had spent ten hours a day or more in his company so he would know that she was there to stay. That he had a home and a life with her forever. Because of her efforts, he had learned to trust her and after a month together, they had started riding as if they had trained together for years. They shared a bond of trust that Violet never wanted to lose. While she was prone to liking every horse she met, she was certain she would never share the same bond with another one as she did with Hawken. No matter how busy she got, she still found a way to spend hours in his company every day.

Halfway into their walk Violet spotted Cassidy making her way across the field. Cassidy was heading in their direction, so Violet decided to stop Hawken's walk. They could head back toward the barn since

Cassidy would pass it on her way to the mess hall to make breakfast for the staff and campers.

"I'd offer you a ride…" Violet said as Cassidy drew near. Violet knew Wade's wife was five months pregnant.

Cassidy batted her hand. "You sound like my husband. Though in his defense, I have been really tired this time around." She reached Violet and they started walking together. "But if Wade had his way, I think he'd wrap me in Bubble Wrap and make me stay in bed until she's born."

"She?" Violet smiled at the woman. "I had heard a rumor that you guys weren't going to find out the gender."

Cassidy shook her head. "Oh, Wade *tried* to float the idea of waiting until the baby was born to know but I told him, look buddy, thanks to you I've had enough surprises in my life lately—I don't need another one." She shrugged. "I had to know. I like planning. And it was still a surprise, just an earlier one."

"That's exciting. I mean, it was always exciting but I'm sure you're happy to start buying things for her and decorating her room. Have you guys thought of any names yet?"

"So far Piper has submitted the names Lumpy or Squirmy for consideration." Cassidy laughed. "Thankfully Wade and I agreed to veto those. I like the name Grace. After everything we've been through, it feels right."

Violet looked away, out across to the horizon. Her eyes burned from the bright sunrise. Or maybe it had more to do with the conversation. Violet would never have what Cassidy enjoyed. She would never have a loving family like they had and would never know what it was like to plan for a child or share jokes with a husband.

The last four years Violet had done everything in her power to prove she was worthy of love. Because if life had taught her one thing it was that no one— not even God—was ever going to be there for her or want her unless she became someone worth wanting. Clearly, just as herself, she wasn't good enough. Why else would He have turned a deaf ear on her childhood pleas for a home, for people who loved her? She had really thought she was getting somewhere with her high standing in the circuits, but then she had been injured. Not one rodeo friend had reached out to her since the season started.

So easily, she had been forgotten.

All over again.

Realizing there had been a long pause, Violet said, "Grace Jarrett. That would be a beautiful name." She cleared her throat. "Speaking of babies, I was over at Boone's last night but forgot to ask him about Silas." The entire reason they had set up the dinner was to brainstorm for the fundraiser for Silas and after the food catastrophe, they had never gotten the evening back on track.

Cassidy sucked in a sharp breath. "I drove out there last weekend. It's so heartbreaking to see his tiny body covered in tubes and wires. Macy can't hold him like a mom should be able to." Cassidy wiped at her eyes. "Rhett and Macy are so battle-weary already. We have to keep praying for them and visiting them so they know they aren't alone in all of this."

Violet dipped her head. She would keep praying but she doubted they would want her to visit. It wasn't as if she was family.

Cassidy glanced her way. "So it sounds like you and Boone have been spending a lot of time together lately?"

Despite the way Cassidy's words made her stomach flip-flop, Violet offered a noncommittal half shrug. "Hazard of working together, I guess."

Cassidy's eyes narrowed. "Inviting you over to dinner isn't work."

Hawken snorted.

"It was Hailey's idea. I care about her, you know that," Violet said.

Then she rested a hand on Hawken's shoulder as they walked. His presence always lent her strength, which she needed right then. Because she probably would have spilled her turmoil of feelings to Cassidy if she hadn't been able to reach out for him. A part of Violet wanted to tell Cassidy that she was attracted to Boone, that she kept finding ways to spend more time around him and loved talking to him. She wanted to tell someone that she had been able to speak to Boone in a raw and honest way and she had never felt that freedom around anyone else in her life.

It terrified her.

But she still wanted to be around him.

It was some silly crush, though, so she'd never

admit anything out loud. She was an orphan whom nobody wanted—definitely not on the level of a Jarrett. And she never would be. Besides, *if* Boone had been interested what would Violet actually bring to the table? No family, no relationship experience and a whole lot of broken pieces. He wouldn't want that, not really. Would never want her. She was around and his family was busy, that was all.

She was fooling herself to even secretly entertain the possibility of more.

At the rodeos she had always had her guard up but she had let it fall at Red Dog Ranch when she let Hailey in. These thoughts about Boone were a by-product of that. Nothing she could trust. She shoved every feeling into the bottom of her heart, cramming them tightly away.

Besides, Boone still loved his wife. He would always love her. Violet could never compare to the woman who had captured Boone's heart all those years ago. And when Violet left, he would forget all about her.

Because everyone always did.

The following weeks flew by quickly. Boone felt as if someone had hit a fast-forward button. Due to staff and volunteer changes, Boone started leading the worship portion of the chapel services along with giving the message. He had been on the worship team at his church during high school and had led worship at summer camp all through college. Since getting married and going to seminary, though, he had hung up his guitar but had always missed it. Those experiences leading worship were what had led him to the desire to be a pastor in the first place.

Boone had convinced Violet to start attending chapel every evening. She would come for the worship portion and sometimes step out mid-message. She never stayed for the final night's service.

Tonight, as the campers filed out of the chapel and counselors wrangled the kids into their cabins, Boone, Violet and Hailey headed toward Boone's bunkhouse. An evening campfire had turned into a tradition for the three of them that they only missed if an emergency sprang up at the ranch that required either Boone's or Violet's attention.

Hailey had hold of both of their hands as she walked between them. "Know what?"

Violet grinned down at her. "What, squirt?"

When he watched Violet interacting with his daughter, he couldn't help the warmth that flooded his chest. Violet wasn't related to them; she didn't have to be kind to an energetic six-year-old. But she was. She seemed to possess boundless patience where Hailey was concerned and displayed a genuine interest in anything his child wanted to talk about or do. That was the thing about Violet that amazed Boone again and again—she cared so much about people. Despite all she had been through and the hurt she had faced in life, her heart was still open, still kind and still full of hope. He admired that about her.

Hailey hopped a few times. "Uncle Wade said he is going to get more horses. Isn't that fun? He said the ranch needs more. I wonder if he'll find one that's my size."

Violet darted a questioning gaze to Boone. Boone sighed. "Wade hasn't mentioned new horses to me, but if he's thinking of getting more, he probably has a plan for them."

Hailey turned pleading eyes toward him. "Can I start riding again?" She tugged on his hand. "I miss it. It's been weeks and I don't want to forget all I learned." She spun toward Violet. "Violet said I was *really* good at it."

Violet let out a breathy laugh. "Guilty as charged." She grimaced. "I mean, she is really good at it, Boone."

Boone glanced between the two of them, his stomach knotting as he did. "Let me think about it."

When they reached his yard, they bypassed the bunkhouse and went right into the backyard. Kodiak was sprawled near the firepit waiting. Her tail thumped the ground when she spotted them.

Hailey ran to Kodiak and hugged her around the neck. Then she looked back at Boone. "I have something else to have you think about, too."

Boone dropped down onto a log to be at her eye level. "Oh? And what's that?"

Hailey wound her fingers together. "Piper and I want to go to the Fourth of July party in town but Aunt Cassidy said she wouldn't be able to be on her feet for that long so they can't take us." She batted her long eyelashes. "Can you?"

Boone rubbed the side of his head. The ranch never

had campers the first week of July because of the holiday so it wasn't as if they would be too busy to attend. "I, ah, that would be a lot. Juggling the two of you all day in such a large crowd. It's just me and I'm not used to—"

"Well, you won't be alone. Violet will come, too." Hailey's gaze shot to Violet. "Won't you?"

Hailey whispered *please, please, please.* Kodiak's brow scrunched as she watched Hailey.

Violet pressed her hands together and rocked forward. "If you guys decide to go, I'm happy to go along." She turned to include Boone in the conversation. "Only if you need help, of course."

Boone pulled Hailey against his chest and kissed the top of her head. "It shouldn't be a problem but let me have a day to think about it and talk to Wade."

After Hailey was in bed, Violet and Boone moved inside to the kitchen table so they could work on the event for Silas. For the last two weeks they had been tossing around ideas for the fundraiser but now that they were entering July and the date was right around the corner, they needed to start making decisions.

Ever faithful, Kodiak followed Boone and lay at his feet.

Violet pulled out her phone. Boone noticed her lock screen was a selfie of her and Hailey. She opened the notes function and scanned over a list she had made. "I know we talked about a design for the flyers and social media ads, but I think the event should have a name."

Boone tugged open a laptop and set it so the screen

faced both of them. "Let's get Rhett and Macy's input. I sent over ideas from the last time we talked, and I want to get their permission to use a picture of Silas." He pressed the button to initiate a video chat with his brother. As they had been planning off and on, Boone had tried to keep Rhett in the loop on anything related to the fundraiser as often as he could.

Rhett's face appeared on the screen, and he gave them a weak smile. He pulled Macy into the frame and she pressed the side of her face against his neck. Boone knew they were trying to stay positive, but he also knew they were walking through the biggest valley of their life and it was draining them.

The second Rhett's voice came through the speakers, Kodiak sprang to her feet and paced around the kitchen, each step punctuated with a loud whine. She swung her head in the direction of the door and waited, then paced back over to Boone, looked at him as if he were deliberately hiding his brother from her and let out a loud bark.

Rhett leaned toward the camera. "Good girl, Kodiak. I'm right here. I sure miss you."

Kodiak zeroed in on the screen. She set her paws on Boone's lap and stood to be eye level with the monitor. Her tail beat a happy pattern against the chair.

Boone looped his arm around her. "She misses you both a lot."

"It's good to see you guys," Rhett said. "Thanks for calling." He glanced off-screen in the direction of the crib bed the hospital had for Silas. "He's sleeping right now. For the most part it was a quiet day here."

Macy nodded. "Keep praying. It's so hard to cling to hope right now." She swiped away a tear as Rhett's arm came around her shoulder. "You know, people usually have these warm and fluffy thoughts about the word *hope*, but placing ourselves in a position to hope—this is anguish." Her voice trembled. She wiped away more tears. "Having an answer, even a bad one, seems easier than sitting in this waiting period. Than not knowing. If we had an answer at least we could plan, we could *do something*." She fisted a hand, then slowly relaxed her fingers. "But choosing to hope, that leaves us smack-dab in the midst of uncertainty and questioning," she said. "You guys know me." She pressed her hand to her chest. "I'm someone who wants to be able to take instant action, but that's not a choice here." She glanced toward the crib. "Our only choice is to wait and pray and hope. I know that probably sounds bad."

Violet coughed a little. "Not at all. I... I understand what you're saying. More than you know. Choosing to hope is often the most dangerous option. At least, it has been for me."

"It's been hard." Rhett glanced at his wife. "It just feels as if God is only answering us in tiny drips when we'd like an ocean wave. Is that so bad? Because this in-between, the not knowing, that hurts the most right now." He rubbed the palm of his hand against his heart.

Boone prayed as his brother and sister-in-law

talked. Being there, watching their only child fight to stay alive, was more than Boone could imagine. And after what he had been through, that was saying a lot.

He noticed they were all looking to him, all waiting. Rhett might have been older, but he had always come to Boone for advice. Even more so once Boone started seminary. The family looked to Boone for spiritual guidance, a task Boone wasn't sure he was up for any longer. He prayed for the right words anyway.

Boone cleared his throat. "The thing about waves, though, is they could drag you under. Too much of anything can knock us over and leave us drowning. Oceans are big and powerful from the get-go, but drips, drips build into something. Drips become something and while the drips are coming, God builds our faith with each tiny splash in the bucket."

Rhett ran a shaky hand over his jaw. "You're right. I know you're right."

Macy smiled at the camera. "God has our little superhero in His hands. We've seen so many drips already." She nodded. "We just have to hang on."

Violet scooted forward in her seat. "Did you say superhero?"

Macy chuckled and turned a loving look off-screen toward Silas's crib. "That's what all the nurses call him."

Violet latched onto Boone's arm. "That's it. We can call the event the Super Silas fundraiser."

Rhett hugged his wife close and kissed the top of her head. "We love that idea."

Boone ran through the rest of the topics he had wanted to touch on and got permission to use pictures of Silas on social media and in the flyers they were going to leave around town and at Chick-N-More.

As they were wrapping up the conversation, Macy elbowed Rhett, who then started talking. "Before we go, we wanted to say thank you to both of you for all you've done and continue to do for the ranch and for Silas." He looked at Violet. "Especially you, Violet. I know being stuck at our ranch during your rodeo season is not what you planned or wanted. Under the circumstances you could have locked yourself away and refused to help and I would have understood, but you didn't. You stepped up and came to our family's rescue. You have been the greatest blessing to all of us Jarretts during this season and I want you to know there will always be a place for you at Red Dog Ranch."

Violet whispered a trembling *thank you* as they signed off. With her shoulders curving inward, she looked so confused and maybe even a bit afraid. Boone fought the desire to pull her into his arms like he'd done before. Everything in him screamed to protect her, to encourage her, to make sure she understood how strong and kind and beautiful she was. Did she know? Did she see all the wonderful things about herself that he did? On the first day they met she had glared at him and refused to back down but now a kind word from Rhett had made her unsure and quiet. He had to know why.

He settled for placing his hand on her back and

rubbing it in a circle. But when she leaned into his touch, Boone had to admit to himself that he had feelings for Violet Byrd. Strong ones. He had never met anyone like her, and he dreaded the thought of her leaving the ranch someday—leaving him. His gut clenched.

Rhett had offered her a place here; dare he hope she would accept his brother's offer?

Boone kept his voice gentle. "What do you want to do, Violet?" That wasn't the right question. He was trying to ask her what he had failed to ask June. He wanted Violet to be happy and feel fulfilled in her life. Try again. He cleared his throat. "Not right now, I mean, but with your life. What's your dream?" He added quickly, "Do you want to stay at Red Dog Ranch?"

She turned in her chair, her eyes snapping to his. "Stay?" she whispered, and looked down. "I… I—" Violet hugged her stomach. "Dreams don't matter, Boone," she said, regaining her normal confidence. She smoothed her hands over the notes scattered across the tabletop. "I believe in doing the best I can wherever life has me because maybe that's all there will ever be to my life, and it's better to accept that and move on." She fiddled with the curled edge of a piece of paper. "It's a pointless waste of time to hang our hearts on things that will never happen."

Boone put his hand on top of one of hers so it stilled. "Dreams aren't pointless, Violet." He touched her chin, guiding her face back to make eye contact. "*Your* dreams aren't pointless. You don't have to tell me, but know that I care about them, whatever they are."

Her eyes narrowed and she backed out of his touch. "If dreams aren't pointless then what are yours, huh? Is Red Dog Ranch where you want to be forever? Are you living your dream?"

He could tell her that right now, with her, this was a dream he would have been willing to stay in for a long time. Red Dog Ranch could be home if she was there. But he pushed those thoughts away. Sure, he was developing feelings for Violet, but they didn't mean anything. They couldn't. Boone was a lonely, grieving widower who was probably looking for comfort and that was all the feelings accounted for. Besides, even if they were something more, what did he have to offer Violet? A bunch of emotional baggage and an uncertain future. Not exactly top of the pickings. She deserved more. Far better than him.

Violet crossed her arms. "Because if you're not actually following your own advice maybe you shouldn't be doling it out so regularly."

He had learned that Violet threw things out like that when she was trying to protect herself, when a conversation was hitting too close to home. It was her way of keeping people at a distance—run them off before they rejected her. But a few words wouldn't scare Boone away. Someday she'd realize she was safe with him. Free to voice whatever she wanted without him running for the hills. For now, the only way to prove that was to dig in and stay when she expected him to take off.

Boone hooked his arm on the back of his chair as he faced her. "You sure don't hold back. I know I've said it before."

She lifted her chin. "And I'm never going to."

"Good." He leaned close, stopping only inches from her face. "I'd never want you to." His voice was warm.

Violet bit her bottom lip, her green eyes on his. If jumping beans could riot, it felt as if they had chosen his stomach as the location for their party. Nerves jangled up Boone's spine. He could kiss Violet right now and then he would know if she was feeling everything he was. He could get lost in her. But Boone had only ever kissed June, and their first kiss had been as awkward high schoolers. He wasn't sure exactly how to proceed with someone he wasn't certain of.

A heartbeat later Violet pulled away. She let out a shaky breath as she ran a hand over her hair. She turned away from him, back to face the table and all their work for the event.

Boone had waited too long. Been too cautious, as usual.

He sighed. "You asked what my dream was."

"Boone, I was goading you and I shouldn't have been. You don't have to—"

"The thing is," he said, "I don't know what my dream is. For as long as I can remember, my life has been planned out. Get married, have kids, finish seminary, become a pastor." He shrugged. After he and June had gotten married, they'd lived at Red Dog Ranch. They had a few years between high school and college to work on their marriage, and then he had enrolled in college. After undergrad he had dived straight into seminary. They had known getting his master's of divinity would take another four years, so they hadn't dreamed beyond that goal.

"There was never a thought to what I dreamed of doing, just what I thought was the right thing to do and become. Being a minster would make God happy, right?" He laughed but it held no humor. "And if I'm being honest, it terrifies me to think maybe I've been wrong all along. What if I'm not cut out to be a minister? The second my life got hard I doubted everything, so there's a good chance I shouldn't be leading anyone."

Violet took his hand in hers. "I think the fact that you have been real and raw about your heartache and about your struggle with God during your grief actually makes you the perfect guy to become a pastor. People don't need someone perfect leading them, just someone who cares about them and God and stands for the truth." She squeezed his hand. "Boone, the messages you've been giving in chapel?" Violet pressed her fingers against her heart. "They've challenged me and caused me to draw closer to God in a way I never have before. And the way you lead worship with such honesty, it's unlike anything I've ever seen or experienced. It's as if you usher the people in your care right to God's throne room. That's how I know what you're doing is exactly what God wants you to do."

Boone's throat burned. Her words had been full

of healing and grace. They trickled into all the broken places in his heart, filling the gaps. He took in a breath. "What about seminary? I don't want to leave Hailey again." He still had another two years of schooling to finish.

"Why do you have to?"

He ran a hand over his short-cropped hair. "I can't go back to Maine and take care of her on my own with school. I know that's not a possibility."

Her brows lowered. "I have to imagine Texas is chock-full of seminaries. Have you looked into transferring to any in the area so you can finish here? Then Hailey could stay at the ranch and you would still be able to spend as much time with her as you could while finishing your degree." She lifted her hands away from his to weave her fingers together in her lap. "Your family is here so it's the best place for Hailey to be."

But will you be here?

She had solved all his problems and washed his worries down the drain so simply, so logically. It was as if she knew exactly how to speak his language. Boone could have hugged her. Instead, being the chicken he was, he nodded. "Sounds like you've given me a lot to think about."

Violet smiled. "And now it's time to think about Silas." She pulled the laptop close and opened their master file for the event. "I think red and blue are the perfect colors for the flyers. They go with the superhero theme. Oh, what if we encourage people to wear their favorite superhero clothes and kids can wear outfits if they want to? We could even hire a few people to walk around in costumes and advertise that kids can take pictures with them." She blew hair out of her face as she typed quickly. "Another idea could be a vote for their favorite superhero character." She put her hands up, fingers spreading apart. "We could have jars labeled for the top ten and people can vote with money and whatever character has the most money in their jar at the end of the night we can declare the greatest hero ever." She scrunched up her nose. "You're not saying anything. Is it too much?"

Some of her hair had fallen forward during her excited rambling. Boone brushed it back behind her ear. "I love all those ideas. They're perfect."

She gave him a wobbly smile. "I just really care about Silas. Rhett and Macy have been so kind to me. I want this to be an amazing event."

"Because of you, it will be." Being braver, Boone allowed his fingers to trace down the back of her neck until his hand landed gently on her shoulder. "You fit here, Violet." He squeezed her shoulder. "You fit here at Red Dog Ranch."

And with me.

Chapter Seven

Violet checked to make sure both Hailey and Piper were secured in their booster seats before she opened the passenger door. Each of the girls wore festive red, white and blue outfits. Piper sported her normal double braids while Hailey had her long blond hair down with just a ribbon tied like a headband. Boone was tossing the last of their supplies into the trunk of his car when Violet buckled herself in.

Boone climbed into the driver's seat and turned the car on. In a tight-fitting T-shirt, jeans and a blue baseball hat, Boone looked like a downright handsome hometown boy. She wouldn't blame any girl at the Fourth of July celebration for gawking at him. Warmth spread through her chest at the thought that they could all stare, but he would be with Violet. Not that he was *with* her in that way, but strangers wouldn't know. For today, he was hers to pal around with and Violet decided to enjoy that. Besides, there was so much more to Boone than how attractive he

"One Minute" Survey

You get up to **FOUR books** <u>and</u> Mystery Gifts...

Dear Reader,

Your opinions are important to us. So if you'll participate in our fast
and free "One Minute" Survey, **YOU** can pick up to four wonderful
books that **WE** pay for!

As a leading publisher of women's fiction, we'd love to hear from
you. That's why we promise to reward you for completing our
survey.

IMPORTANT: Please complete the survey and return it. We'll send
your Free Books and Free Mystery Gifts right away. **And we pay
for shipping and handling too!** _We pay for_
← EVERYTHING!

Try **Love Inspired® Romance Larger-Print** books and fall in love
with inspirational romances that take you on an uplifting journey of
faith, forgiveness and hope.

Try **Love Inspired® Suspense Larger-Print** books where courage
and optimism unite in stories of faith and love in the face of danger.

Or TRY BOTH!

Thank you again for participating in our "One Minute"
Survey. It really takes just a minute (or less) to complete the
survey… and your free books and gifts will be well worth it!

Sincerely,

Pam Powers

Pam Powers
for Reader Service

"One Minute" Survey

GET YOUR FREE BOOKS AND FREE GIFTS!

✓ Complete this Survey   ✓ Return this survey

▶ DETACH AND MAIL CARD TODAY! ▶

1 Do you try to find time to read every day?
☐ YES   ☐ NO

2 Do you prefer books which reflect Christian values?
☐ YES   ☐ NO

3 Do you enjoy having books delivered to your home?
☐ YES   ☐ NO

4 Do you find a Larger Print size easier on your eyes?
☐ YES   ☐ NO

YES! I have completed the above "One Minute" Survey. Please send me my Free Books and Free Mystery Gifts (worth over $20 retail). I understand that I am under no obligation to buy anything, as explained on the back of this card.

☐ I prefer Love Inspired* Romance Larger Print 122/322 IDL GNTG
☐ I prefer Love Inspired* Suspense Larger Print 107/307 IDL GNTG
☐ I prefer BOTH 122/322 & 107/307 IDL GNTS

FIRST NAME	LAST NAME

ADDRESS

APT.#	CITY

STATE/PROV.	ZIP/POSTAL CODE

© 2019 HARLEQUIN ENTERPRISES ULC
" and ® are trademarks owned by Harlequin Enterprises ULC. Printed in the U.S.A.

Offer limited to one per household and not applicable to series that subscriber is currently receiving.
Your Privacy—The Reader Service is committed to protecting your privacy. Our Privacy Policy is available online at www.ReaderService.com or upon request from the Reader Service. We make a portion of our mailing list available to reputable third parties that offer products we believe may interest you. If you prefer that we not exchange your name with third parties, or if you wish to clarify or modify your communication preferences, please visit us at www.ReaderService.com/consumerschoice or write to us at Reader Service Preference Service, P.O. Box 9062, Buffalo, NY 14240-9062. Include your complete name and address.

LI/SLI-520-OM20

was, and Violet knew him—really knew him—and that was something she had over anyone who tried to catch his eye.

The memory of Boone's fingers skimming her neck and of him leaning in close played through her mind. She had thought he was going to kiss her.

Had hoped he would.

Foolish, overactive imagination.

Violet smoothed her hands over her skirt, wondering if the white dress and boots had been too much for their outing.

Boone caught her eye and winked. "You look really pretty."

Piper crinkled a bag of cheese crackers in the back seat. "Like *super* pretty." She kicked the back of Boone's seat as he maneuvered the car off the ranch's property. "Kinda like out of a magazine. My mom says they change the way those girls look on a computer." She loudly munched her crackers. "But there's no computer here and you're pretty like those covers so I'm going to tell my mom that."

Hailey nodded along. "You're as pretty as a sunset. Do you know sunsets are Dad's favorite?"

Violet's heart felt as if it could burst. She thanked God for bringing these two sweet little girls into her life. "If you two keep talking like that I might just have to keep you around forever." She caught Piper's gaze in the rearview mirror. "Speaking of your mom, how's she feeling today?"

"She said it feels like the baby's celebrating the Fourth with a party in her belly," Piper said matter-offactly. "But don't worry." She held up a hand. "Dad is like a bee buzzing around her. That's what my mom says. So she'll be good. He makes sure of it. Because of love and stuff."

Boone found a radio station that was playing kid-friendly music and the girls started singing along. Violet was sure the back of his car would be coated in a layer of cracker crumb dust by the time they reached the town square, but Boone didn't seem to mind.

Boone hooked his hand on the top of the steering wheel. "Are you already regretting coming along with this excitable crew?"

Violet relaxed into her seat. "Actually, I'm really looking forward to going to the fair and seeing the fireworks. I'm always in a rodeo on the Fourth, so I've never just been able to enjoy being at a celebration before."

Boone rolled his shoulders. "Do you miss it? The rodeo, I mean."

"Parts of it." She shrugged. "I guess I miss doing something I'm good at. And I love riding Hawken at shows. He really comes alive in front of a crowd." She sighed. "Who am I kidding, I do miss riding. That was all I knew for so long so it's a part of me."

"You're good at this." Boone glanced her way and jerked his head back toward the girls. "You're amazing with kids, Violet. And you've blown all of us away at the ranch with your ability to plan and the creative ways you approach problems." He laid his arm on the center console with his hand palm-up. An invitation? Violet hardly knew. "Don't sell yourself short, that's all I'm saying. You're good at many things." His elbow nudged hers. "And you'll ride again. Hawken will be good as new. I've seen the town veterinarian in the barn checking him every week and Carter will make sure Hawken is up to speed once he gets back."

When they reached the fairgrounds located on the far edge of the town, they decided to leave the camp chairs, blankets and other things for the fireworks in the car while they wandered through the booths and enjoyed some of the games and rides being offered at the small carnival. After Boone paid their entry fees, Hailey and Piper immediately tugged them to the Tilt-A-Whirl, where the four of them piled into a single red car. Boone and Violet ended up in the middle with a girl on either side. When the ride began, their little car went up and started to spin wildly. Violet latched onto Boone's arm while both girls tossed their hands into the air and laughed.

"I forgot how twirly these things could be." Violet leaned toward Boone and spoke loud enough to be heard over the girls' happy screams and the ride's grinding gears. "A little scarier than I remember."

Boone slipped his arm around her waist and tugged her flush to his side. "You're safe. I've got you."

They spent the rest of the afternoon hopping from ride to ride and cheering one another on at every game booth. Piper won a large stuffed octopus that could be worn as a hat. She proudly slung it around by one of its legs. Boone held Piper's other hand and Violet had Hailey by the hand. Boone and Violet walked close enough that their shoulders kept bumping. It made sense to stick near to one another in such a large crowd.

Boone grinned down at Piper. "You could name him Calamari."

"Oh, wait, I have a good one." Violet laughed. "How about Billy the Squid?"

Piper squinted at them. "I don't know why that's so funny, but he already has a name. This is Scuba Doo." She lofted the maroon-and-green-striped hat-stuffed animal hybrid into the air and then slammed him onto her head. As she walked, his eight little legs wobbled around her. "The great crime-fighting octopus."

At one point while they were watching Hailey throw darts at moving balloons, Violet got choked up. Never in her life had she experienced such a carefree and fun day spent with people who seemed to enjoy having her around. Who each seemed to genuinely *want* her to be there. Is this what her life would have been like if her parents hadn't died in the car accident? She had been six when her parents died, so she didn't remember much, but the memories she did have of her parents were happy ones. Would they have continued on to be like this?

Violet would never know.

Because that would never be her life.

But today, with these three, she could pretend they were her family. She could enjoy a taste of everything she had missed out on for so many years. It wouldn't last, but that night she planned to tuck the memory of today somewhere safe in her heart so she could pull it out and relive it in her mind whenever she felt alone. Because even if the day ended right now, between the smiles Boone kept sending her way and the girls' obvious joy, today had already been the most perfect day of Violet's life.

While they waited in a long line for banana split funnel cakes and cotton candy lemonade, Violet couldn't help but thank God. *And not just for today, Lord, but for the accident at the rodeo, for making me take a pause in my life to reconnect with You and learn that maybe it's okay to trust other people. Maybe You have bigger plans for my life than just being alone on the circuit.* Earlier, Boone had wrapped his arm around her and told her she was safe. And for the first time since before her parents died, she knew she was…with him. He was so thoughtful and good, and she couldn't imagine him ever hurting her. She snuck a peek at Boone as he pulled his wallet from his back pocket and paid for their sugary treats. *Thank You for Boone, God. I know it's just for a season and he's not mine but thank You for using him to show me that good men exist. That maybe my hope for a family, for someone to care about me and want to be with me, isn't all in vain.*

Hope tiptoed into her heart while she prayed, and it wasn't the heavy draining sort she was so used to. This hope felt light, free.

Yet just as tenuous as the other kind. While the heavy hope chipped away at her sometimes, she knew this light kind had the power to do much worse. It could shatter her heart into so many tiny pieces, she might never be able to put it back together if it broke.

After the girls downed their drinks and funnel cake, Boone checked his watch. "We have thirty minutes before the rodeo starts and once we're done with that, I think we should stake out our spots for the fireworks show."

Hailey pointed toward the Ferris wheel. "We have to do that." Everyone else agreed. When they reached the Ferris wheel, they had to split into two groups, an adult with each child. Hailey picked to ride with Violet. Piper and Boone were in the car in front of theirs and as the ride twisted them higher, Piper whooped and made their seat swing a little.

Hailey swallowed hard. "Can I hold your hand while we go up? I'm not as brave as Piper."

"Of course, squirt." Violet's heart squeezed and she gathered Hailey to her side. She reached over and held her hand, too.

Hailey scooted even closer. "Sometimes I can't breathe when I'm scared." She touched her chest. "And it hurts here."

A panic attack? Violet tightened her hold on the little girl. "Has it always been that way?"

Hailey shook her head. "Just since Mom."

Did Boone know? Violet would have to say something to him, just in case. She didn't want Hailey trying to handle something like that all on her own.

Violet smoothed a hand over Hailey's head. "You can *always* hold my hand, okay? You never even have to ask. And Hailey?" She waited until the girl looked at her. "You're incredibly brave. You've been through so much this year and look at you, out living and having so much fun. I think your mom is so proud of you. I know I am."

Hailey clung to Violet a little harder. "If that makes me brave, then you're the bravest of us all." She rubbed the toe of her shoe back and forth along the plastic seat. "Both your parents died but you're happy and love people." She rested her head on Violet's arm. "You probably make them super proud, too."

Violet's eyes burned. She bit her lip and hugged Hailey tighter as they crested the top of the wheel.

Hailey snuggled in her arms. "Do you like my daddy?"

Violet stiffened at the question but instantly forced her body to relax again so Hailey wouldn't pick up on her reaction. "Of course I like him. Your dad is so nice he makes it impossible not to be his friend. Even when I tried not to like him in the beginning."

Hailey shook her head and straightened in her seat. "Not like a friend." She spread out her fingers. Her eyes widened in emphasis. "*More* than a friend. Do you want to marry him?"

A nervous laugh left Violet's lips. How many times did these wheels go around? "Hailey, sweetheart, your dad and I are just friends. We don't know each other enough to get married and we're not… It's not like that, okay? Your dad is a great guy and I'm, well, I'm just…" *Not good enough. No one has ever wanted me. He's a Jarrett and the Jarretts are amazing and I don't belong with them.* Violet shrugged.

This wasn't a talk she needed to have with a six-year-old.

Hailey skewed her mouth to the side. "You're just what?"

Violet flipped her hand in the direction of the rodeo arena. "What I do for a living is dangerous and we both know your dad doesn't like that. And my job takes me traveling all over and your dad likes things set in a schedule and wants to be a pastor with roots at a church somewhere. He wouldn't want my life. Even if…" Violet blew out a long stream of air. "It would never work."

Hailey shrugged. "Aunt Shannon went to another country with Uncle Carter. People do that. Dad talks to them. He said they're happy."

"That's because your aunt Shannon really likes Carter. She doesn't want to be without him so she's willing to do that." Violet gripped the edge of the cart but the warm metal offered no comfort. "No one's ever been willing to come after me." She forced a smile because she didn't want Hailey to pick up on how much the conversation was twisting her insides. "People have to want you in their lives forever to do that and that's just not how things are for me."

Hailey poked her ribs. "Well, he likes you. My dad."

Violet sucked in a sharp breath and darted a look toward the car Boone and Piper occupied. She ran her hands over her hair. "Did he tell you that?"

"Naw." Hailey hooked her hands over the metal lap bar. "But I know. He looks at you all soft and warm. It's the same way he looked at my mom. He doesn't ever look that way at other people. I've only seen him look that way at Mom, pork belly sandwiches and blueberry smoothies."

Pork belly sandwiches. She'd have to remember that tidbit of information.

Violet tried to hide her smile. "I'm happy to know I rate up there with blueberry smoothies."

"He *loves* them." Hailey pointed a finger at her when she said *loves*. "They're his favorite thing ever. Like he pretends to drool when he sees one." Hailey scrunched up her face. "I'm glad he doesn't pretend to drool around you, though. That would be weird."

Thankfully the ride ended then and Violet was saved from more awkward talk about Boone. Everything Hailey said made Violet's stomach do flip-flops, but she could hardly take love advice from a six-year-old.

When they joined the rest of the group Boone already had Piper's hand. Hailey latched onto Violet and then Boone reached over and laced his fingers with Violet's other hand.

"To the rodeo?" he asked in an easy manner.

As if he wasn't holding her hand—her heart— in his.

She opened her mouth, closed it, opened it again.

Hailey jabbed her elbow into Violet's leg, causing Violet to look her way. Hailey dramatically winked up at her.

Maybe a six-year-old knew better after all.

The mingled smells of fried foods, too many people pressed together on a hot day and livestock was

exactly what Boone remembered from the many times
he had accompanied his dad to rodeos when he was
younger. For some reason the scents made Boone
relax because they reminded him of home and childhood. Maine had been beautiful, and the seafood was
beyond compare, but he had missed all this in the
years he'd been gone.

He didn't want to leave again.

Thanks to Violet's sound advice, he probably
wouldn't have to. After she suggested he could finish his degree at a nearby seminary, Boone had gone
home that night and started researching programs in
Texas. There was more than one good option within
an hour of the ranch. The next day he had phoned his
adviser in Maine and they had discussed what transferring would look like and how his credits could be
affected. A new school may not honor all the courses
he had completed, but it was a small price to pay to
stay near his family and maintain his role in Hailey's life.

Boone made sure Hailey and Piper were comfortable in the stands as they waited for the rodeo to
begin. They both had their hands stuffed into a large
bag of cinnamon popcorn. He chided himself for all
the sweets he was letting them eat; Piper would probably be jumping off the walls by the time he got her
home to her parents. Then again, today was a special
occasion. Truly, Boone had always been a strict parent and six months ago he wouldn't have allowed the
girls to indulge so much. But he was learning that life
was short and it could change rapidly so it was more

than okay to have days to celebrate spending time with people he cared about and having fun.

One over-sugared day was worth the memories.

Besides, they *had* eaten hot dogs at some point during the day, so he was counting that as a win.

Country music blared through the loudspeakers and a team of women on horseback cantered into the arena, all holding flags. Everyone in the stands rose as someone took the stage to sing the anthem.

When the song ended, Hailey jumped up and down, pointing at the horsewomen getting ready to begin their routine. "Oh! Look at them, they're all so beautiful." She wound her hands together and pressed them against her collarbone. "I wish I could do that someday." She glanced at Boone and the bright smile that had lit her face vanished immediately. She dropped her hands and scuffed her shoe against the bleachers. "But I can't. I know. You say I can't." She turned a longing gaze back toward the women riding in formation. "I just wish..." She sighed.

Boone crouched beside her and placed a hand on her shoulder. He wanted to kick himself. He had allowed his fears to crush his daughter's dreams. "You really want to learn to ride, don't you?"

She blinked away tears. "Yes, but you said no. A lot. So I can't."

Boone placed his hands gently on either side of her face so he was cradling his precious child's head. "I want you to start riding again." He gestured toward the arena. "Someday I want to be in these stands watching you out there."

Hailey eyed him as if he might be pulling a prank on her. "But you said it was dangerous."

Boone rubbed his jaw. "It is dangerous, but that doesn't mean you shouldn't do it." And he would worry and fret and debate with himself every time she fell off a horse, but he would let her do it because this was a part of growing—both for her and him. "Do you love riding, Hailey?"

She nodded enthusiastically.

"Then I want you to ride."

She grabbed his hand and jiggled it. "You mean it? I can really go back to riding?"

Boone scooped her into his arms for a tight hug. "I mean it." He kissed the top of her head. "I love you, Hailey. I love you so much."

"I love you, too, Daddy."

He set her back down and she scampered to Piper and told her she could ride again. She and Piper joined hands and broke into a triumphant dance that would have put many football players' end zone moves to shame. The stuffed octopus on Piper's head flopped its arms each time she moved, making it appear as if Scuba Doo was as happy over the news as they were.

Violet bumped her shoulder into his. "You did good, Mr. Dad."

He let out a rattling breath. "It's really hard, the letting go part of parenting. I didn't think it would hit me this hard at six."

"I'm pretty sure it's a lifelong process." She glanced over at the girls and she had so much warmth and love reflecting in her eyes, Boone had to remind himself to take a breath. "But I've heard that it means you're doing your job right." She patted his arm.

Once the beginning routine was done, everyone sat back down. Violet shielded her eyes against the bright evening sun as she tried to watch. At the edge of her seat, leaning forward, she was soaking it all in.

The rodeo.

Her home.

Her life.

She would leave him for it again someday. Boone would lose her, too.

Boone swallowed past the lump in his throat as he tugged off his baseball hat and plunked it onto her head. "There. Now your arm doesn't have to get tired."

She readjusted the hat and then turned his way. "You sure?" She tapped the bill.

Boone's mouth went dry. Violet was a gorgeous woman, but she looked incredibly adorable wearing his hat. She looked...she looked like the woman he wanted by his side.

Eyes narrowing, Violet tilted her head. Then she grinned and tapped his chest with a finger. "Earth to Boone, are you there?"

He smiled and took her hand, lacing their fingers together. Boone scooted closer to her. "I'm here." He jutted his chin toward the arena. "Barrels are first. Do you wish you were riding tonight?"

"No. Not this time." Her voice was breathy. "I'm happy here. In the stands for once, that's what I mean."

Boone nodded. "Wade says the new horses are arriving at the ranch tomorrow. He told me he asked you to look them over for him and help decide which ones should be used for the kids and trail rides and which ones can be workhorses for our staff."

Violet looked down at their joined hands and smiled in a small, cute way. "I'm looking forward to getting to ride again, though none of them will be as good as Hawken." She winked.

When they had been walking through the crowd, Boone had reached for Violet's hand automatically. Force of habit. He had done it countless times when Hailey, June and he had been out anywhere. At the fair he had tried to convince himself the action was nothing more than instinct—he didn't want their group to get lost and he was used to holding some-one's hand.

But there was no danger of Violet getting lost while they were sitting side by side in the stands. Boone looked down at their joined hands and sud-denly a huge wave of guilt crashed through him. What was he doing? His wife had only died months ago. He had loved June and he wanted to honor her memory. It was disrespectful to move on so soon.

Wasn't it?

A sick feeling churned his stomach. It felt like he was cheating, like he was doing something horribly wrong. And maybe he was—well, not cheating, but wasn't he leading Violet on? He needed to focus on Hailey and he had already admitted that he had noth-ing to offer a woman like Violet. He was a grieving and broken man and it wasn't Violet's job to fix him or help him. He had plans for school, but after that he had no clue what he would be doing. Rhett would return to the ranch eventually so there wouldn't be a place for Boone forever. A chapel speaker was only needed at Red Dog Ranch during the summer.

Violet, don't you want to be with me? I just lost my wife and am still dealing with that grief, I have a child who would need lots of attention from any woman I end up with, oh, and I have no means of supporting us and no idea if I'll ever actually have anything be-yond school debt from my degrees. I'm also training to be a pastor, yet I keep tripping in my own walk with God—but you knew that part.

He was a winner, all right.

Boone let go of Violet's hand and inched away from her a little. "Going to find the men's room." An excuse, plain and simple, but Boone needed air away from Violet where he could think. "You've got the girls?"

Unaware of his shift in mood, Violet offered a heart-robbing smile and gave him a thumbs-up. Her smile made his chest ache. He wanted to forget all the thoughts he had just had so he could sit back down and take her hand again.

Instead, Boone turned and forced himself to take the stairs two at a time.

Chapter Eight

Violet spread the blanket onto the ground while Boone set up the two camp chairs he had declared were for the old folks of the group when Hailey and Piper tried to lay claim to them. The girls recovered from their disappointment in record time, dashing around the field to chase the lightning bugs that could be found this close to the river.

Violet kept glancing at Boone, trying to read his mood. For most of the day he had seemed completely relaxed, but at the rodeo he had suddenly grown quiet. Did he regret telling Hailey she could ride again? Violet raked through their conversations and tried to land on anything she might have said or done to upset him but couldn't think of anything. Or was he simply tired and being out in the sun all day had finally worn him down?

Whatever it was, she was having a hard time understanding. During the course of the day Boone had gone from friendly to flirty. He had held her hand multiple times and had said some things that made her want to beg him to kiss her already.

Hadn't Boone once joked that he was born to be mild? More like born to be the most confusing man on earth.

Boone groaned as he eased into his chair. Violet had given him back his hat after the rodeo and she had to admit he looked adorable wearing it. "I think I've been in school for too long. I'm not used to being on my feet like that all day."

"You did say you were an old man, right?" Violet teased.

Boone offered a weak smile in response. Something was definitely on his mind, but with the fireworks show starting in less than ten minutes and the girls nearby, now probably wasn't the time to press him. And it wasn't the right time to bring up Hailey's confessions about her panic attacks, either. Violet would tell him tonight after Hailey was in bed.

She walked on her knees toward the other chair and fished a small soft-sided cooler from where it had been stowed. When they picked up Piper from her house that morning, Cassidy had thrust the bag into their hands. She unzipped the bag and started pulling out the treats Boone's sister-in-law had packed. A few small cans of Dr Pepper, homemade tortilla chips and salsa, small containers of blueberry cobbler and four baggies full of puppy chow, which happened to be one of Violet's favorite treats. She loved the combination of Chex cereal, peanut butter, chocolate and powdered sugar and couldn't remember the last time she had eaten it. The foster mom at the first house she had been placed in used to make it almost weekly. During those first few months, the special treat had been the only thing that was able to draw Violet from her room.

The only thing that made her flashbacks of the accident stop.

Not wanting to relive those moments, Violet set the baggies away. "Cassidy sure goes all out." Violet found some cutlery and decorative napkins in the bag. "Not that any of us need more goodies." She laid her hand over her abdomen. "I'm still stuffed from all the fried food at the fair."

Boone rested his elbows on his knees and leaned forward. "Do I see blueberry cobbler?" He rubbed his hands together like an excited kid.

Violet handed him a fork and one of the small containers. "I heard through the grapevine that you had a thing for blueberries."

Boone dug right in. "They're better than candy."

Piper and Hailey joined them a few minutes later.

"There are just too many lightning bugs." Piper let out a loud breath as she dropped onto the blanket. It was difficult to take her seriously with Scuba Doo's tentacles uncontrollably wobbling around her face.

Hailey joined Piper on the blanket, shaking her head. "We could never catch them all. But we did try very hard." She wheezed as she caught her breath. They would both sleep well tonight.

An announcement sounded, letting everyone know the fireworks were about to start.

Violet tugged her phone from her back pocket. "I promised Cassidy I'd send her some pictures, but we've been bad about taking them." Because they had been having too much fun. They had only succeeded in snapping a shot of Piper and Hailey faking being sick after the Tilt-A-Whirl and one of Piper wearing her octopus hat. It was about time to snap some group photos. "Let's all squeeze together for a selfie."

The girls piled onto Violet's lap, almost knocking her over with their eagerness. Boone took off his baseball hat and smoothed his hands over his hair. Then he crouched in the background behind Violet so he could be in the picture, but he was almost cut out of the frame.

Before Violet could take the picture, Hailey scowled at the image on the phone. "Dad, you have the longest arms so you should hold the phone."

Boone raised his eyebrows and looked to Violet, silently asking permission. She handed over her phone. Boone started to stretch his arm out, but Hailey stopped him again.

"You look weird with just your head in the background behind Violet," Hailey said. She skewed her mouth to the side for a few seconds. "You should put your other arm around her like you're hugging her from behind." Boone only hesitated a second before draping his arm over Violet's collarbone so he could rest his hand on her shoulder. It brought the side of his face in contact with hers. Hailey smiled brightly. "Perfect! See? It's so much better. You can take the picture now."

"Well, since I have your permission." He chuckled, his warm breath tickling Violet's cheek. Boone took three pictures. "Just in case," he announced.

When his arm unwound from Violet, she missed its weight and warmth. A shiver ran up her spine. The first firework burst in the air, bright orange against the night sky. A family nearby started to clap.

"You girls stand facing me and I'll take one with a firework going off behind you. Then your parents can see some of the show." They obeyed and he snapped a handful of shots.

Finally, Hailey snatched the phone from her dad. "Now you and Violet with the fireworks."

Boone got up and offered Violet his hand. She took it and he pulled her to her feet. He had tugged with more strength than necessary, so she bumped against him, almost falling over. She laughed and tilted her head up as her free hand came to land on his chest in search of support. But they were so close that when she looked up her nose grazed Boone's and a heartbeat later his lips were on hers. Violet's arms went around him instinctively, her fingers tracing across the strong back muscles she had admired for weeks. Boone's hand slipped through her hair so he was cradling her head and, in that moment, safe in his arms, Violet believed she might have been the most cherished woman in the world. Boone deepened the kiss and Violet rose on her tiptoes to follow suit. This kiss, his kiss, was everything. It was home and acceptance and protection all rolled into one beautiful moment that Violet never wanted to stop.

The cheers of two very excited little girls broke them apart.

Boone sprang away from her. He looked from Hailey, to Violet, back to Hailey. "I'm sorry. I'm so sorry," he said, but Violet wasn't sure which one of them he was talking to. Was he worried about what his daughter might think? Or was he sorry he had kissed Violet?

Hailey lifted Violet's phone. "I took pictures of it." She swiped through the screen showing frame after frame of Violet and Boone kissing. "I like this one the most." She shoved the phone into Violet's face. The image captured them kissing with three fireworks bursting perfectly behind them. "That one's totally framable." Hailey tapped the phone.

Violet glanced over at Boone, but he was studying the ground, his hand cupping the back of his neck. She wished she could tell if he was embarrassed or just unsure. When Violet was finally able to wrangle her phone from Hailey's grasp, she tucked it safely away even though she really wanted to get a better look at the pictures. Her phone vibrated with a text but she decided it was probably better to ignore it until she got home. Otherwise it might appear as if she was instantly texting someone about what had happened.

Piper stared at them with an open mouth. "Are you two getting married?"

"No," Boone and Violet said in unison.

"But you *kissed*," Piper yelled the word, drawing attention from fireworks watchers seated around them. A lady surrounded by children on a blanket in front of theirs couldn't hide her amusement.

Boone moved both his hands in a keep-it-down motion. "That doesn't always mean what you think it means, okay?" He pointed toward the sky. "Watch the show."

Hailey jabbed Piper in the ribs. "But we already saw *the show*." They both dissolved into a fit of giggles that even the booms of bursting fireworks couldn't cover up.

Violet and Boone glanced at each other and both let out laughs that were clearly tinged with nerves. They needed to talk, but in front of the girls wasn't the appropriate time.

When the show ended, everyone in the crowd got to their feet and started making their way to the parking lot. Boone and Violet gathered the bag, blanket and chairs and each took a girl by the hand before pressing into the crowd.

Violet's stomach was in knots. She had enjoyed their kiss and didn't want it to be their last but she had to know what Boone was thinking. When the girls seemed distracted enough, she brushed up against his side. "Hey, are you okay?"

Boone met her gaze. "I'm good. How about you?"

"I'm fine," Violet said slowly, relief ebbing through the muscles in her shoulders.

Piper yawned loudly. "Well, I'm tired and my legs hurt. Thanks for asking."

"That's a subtle hint if I ever heard one." Boone

chuckled as he hauled his niece into his arms. Violet eased the camp chairs from his hold and slung them over her shoulder.

Hailey lifted her arms toward Boone. "Hold me, too, Daddy."

Violet divested Boone of the bag and blanket so both of his arms were free.

He scanned over the jumble of items in her arms. "You sure you're okay to carry all that?"

Violet gave him a quick salute. "I'll make it. Besides, your cargo is far more precious." She smiled softly, watching him as he scooped up Hailey with tender care. The little girls each laid their heads on his shoulders, closing their eyes as he carried them through the crowd. They had complete trust in Boone, that he was strong enough to support them and protect them. They could relax in his arms, knowing he was there and he would take care of whatever came their way.

It made Violet think about how God is often referred to in the Bible as a father to believers. Because of the circumstances of her upbringing, Violet had never clung to that idea of God. She had no frame of reference to apply it to her relationship—did God care for her and hold her and protect her like Boone did with Hailey and Piper? Violet allowed her steps to fall a few behind Boone's. She looked up at the sky and whispered a prayer. "Hold me, too."

Violet caught back up with her group. Already lost in sleep, Hailey's mouth was hanging open. The arms of Piper's octopus hat bobbed in time with each of Boone's steps. The scene caused Violet's heart to squeeze with longing. Boone was such a gentle and caring father. Even though she had valid reasons in the beginning, she was now having a hard time believing she had ever doubted him.

Between the way he cared for kids, his dedication to his extended family, how he encouraged her and the intensity in his kiss, Violet felt as if she might have finally found home. She loved this man who was a mix of book smarts, physical strength and a compassionate heart.

She loved him.

Violet's foot caught on a lump in the field and she tripped a little. Boone spun, obviously wanting to help but there wasn't much he could do without dropping one of the girls—which he would never do.

"If you want to, you can set everything down and I can come back for it all while you wait with the girls in the car," he offered.

Violet shook her head. She had never been more thankful for the pitch-dark of night because it felt as if her body was on fire, and in the daylight Boone would have noticed her turning every shade of red.

Boone leaned closer, his gaze inspecting her face. "Are you sure you're okay? Your eyes," he whispered. "Don't take offense, but you look like a spooked horse."

Of course she did. She had just realized she was in love.

With him.

She sucked in a sharp breath. "Just tired, I guess."

And it wasn't a lie because Violet was tired—tired of living with her guard up, tired of being alone. She was so thankful that Boone had been able to charm the guards stationed around her heart and had been able to stroll right in to take up residence.

On the drive home they only spoke a few times, sharing what was their favorite firework in the show and quietly chuckling over something one of the girls did or said that day. Both Hailey and Piper snored the whole ride back to Red Dog Ranch.

Boone drove his car straight over the grass to Violet's bunkhouse.

"Boone," she whispered. "You'll ruin the grass."

"Not just once." He shook his head. "Either way, I don't think my brother would mind. You did say you were tired."

Violet opened her door as quietly as she could. "Well, good night."

"Violet." Boone's voice was unsure. She glanced back at him. "I had a really nice time with you today."

Violet nodded. "I did, too." She shut the door and he drove back to the driveway so he could head to the other side of the ranch where Wade's house was located. When his car was long gone, Violet let out a happy squeal and then ran into her house. She closed the door and leaned her back against it as she found her phone and finally checked the message waiting there.

A text from Cassidy: Wait. Hold up. You and my brother-in-law? I can't believe this.

Violet's eyes landed on the text preceding Cassidy's

message. It was the picture of Boone and Violet kissing with the three fireworks exploding behind them. The one Hailey had dubbed framable.

Violet groaned. "Hailey." And she slumped down the door. She pressed the edge of her phone to her chin and tried to blink away the tears that quickly gathered in her eyes. Cassidy's text held no excitement or welcome. *I can't believe this.* Actually, it sounded as if she were upset. Of course, Boone's family would be.

No one had ever wanted Violet, not for the long haul. She hadn't been good enough for her own aunt and uncle or any of the foster families. No matter how hard she tried to prove her worth to others, everyone ended up finding her lacking.

Hadn't Boone said a kiss doesn't always mean what someone thought it meant? With that statement, he might as well have yelled that he didn't actually care about Violet, she was just there and convenient and he was lonely. She fisted her hands in her hair.

She had so badly wanted him to care, wanted to be good enough, that she had missed all the signs. *How stupid.*

The Jarretts were an amazing family. Pillars of the town of Stillwater and well respected in the larger foster community throughout Texas. If her own family hadn't wanted her, there was no way Violet could ever be good enough to warrant Boone's romantic attention. The Jarretts were the ideal family, and no matter how hard she tried, Violet would never belong in their ranks.

And Cassidy knew it. Which meant Wade knew, too. How could she face them again?

You and my brother-in-law? I can't believe this.

Violet had never felt like such a fool. Her plea to God earlier felt silly, too. *Hold me.* She wasn't a cute child like Piper or Hailey. Violet was damaged, discarded goods. No one treasured discounted merchandise.

She laid her head on her knees and finally let herself cry.

Wade must have been watching for Boone because he was out the door and down the porch steps before Boone had a chance to throw the gearshift into Park. Boone's gaze went to the clock embedded in his dashboard and he grimaced. He was getting Piper home late, but Wade had to know they didn't start fireworks until it was dark outside.

Wade tugged open his door. "You grab Hailey and I'll carry Piper in."

Boone scrunched his brow. "You can just lift Piper out and I'll head home with Hailey. They're both asleep." There was no need to chance waking Hailey by moving her in and out of the car.

Wade shook his head. "No can do, bud. Cassidy insists that you come inside. She said I wasn't allowed to come back in without you. So, come on, man. You wouldn't want to upset my pregnant wife, would you?" He motioned for Boone to get out of the car. "Hailey can sleep with Piper in her room."

Boone sighed and climbed out of the car.

Wade opened the door where Piper was and stifled a laugh. "What is that thing on her head? I mean, I saw it in the picture, but…wow."

"Scuba Doo, obviously, the crime-fighting octopus," Boone deadpanned.

"Oh, right. *Obviously.*" Wade grinned at him. "Thanks for taking her along today. From the couple pictures you guys sent it looked like everyone was having a good time." He nudged Boone as he passed with Piper in his arms. "You included."

Wing Crosby, a large white goose, honked from the top of the steps leading up to Wade's porch.

Wade grunted at the goose. "You do that again and wake up my kid and I *will* put you on the table for Thanksgiving."

Cassidy opened the front door. "Oh, stop. We all know you secretly love that bird because it makes you think of Shannon."

Wing shook his tail feathers and honked again.

"You think I'm kidding, but I'm not," Wade said, affection clear in his voice.

The goose had been hand-raised by their sister, Shannon, who had forced Wade to pinkie-promise to take care of him until she returned. Being twins, Wade and Shannon had always been close.

Boone tipped his head to Cassidy as she held the door for both men. He followed Wade upstairs, tugged off Hailey's shoes and laid her next to Piper in the queen-size bed.

"They're going to sleep hard," Boone whispered. Wade chuckled and nodded.

At the bottom of the stairs, Cassidy tapped her toe on the hardwood floor. When Boone tried to step past her, she snagged his arm. "Not so fast, Romeo." She steered him toward a leather reclining chair and pressed on his shoulders, encouraging him to sit. "You've got some explaining to do."

Cloudstorm, Piper's gray-and-white cat, leaped to the back of Boone's chair. The cat's tail curled onto Boone's shoulder as it started purring. Being leery of cats, Boone leaned forward in the chair, away from Cloudstorm. The cat yawned loudly and proceeded to claim more of the headrest.

"Someone's going to have to help me here. What am I supposed to be explaining?" Boone looked to Wade but his little brother only shrugged.

Cassidy lowered herself onto the coffee table a few feet away, picked up her cell phone and shoved it toward Boone. "Let's start with this."

Everything clicked into place when Boone saw the image displayed there. It was him and Violet kissing at the fireworks show. Lost in their embrace, Violet looked breathtaking. Boone's mouth went dry. "She sent this to you?"

What would have motivated Violet to do that?

"I sent her a text right after I got it because I was excited but she never responded." Cassidy took back her phone. She fanned herself. "I have to give it to you—it looks like it was one great kiss." Then his sister-in-law pinned him with a stare. "But listen, I like Violet a lot and I don't want to see her get hurt. And I don't think you would on purpose but you might without realizing it." She arched an eyebrow. "How long has this been going on?"

Boone scrubbed his hand over his face and let out a long breath. "Only today. It was a onetime thing."

Cassidy rolled her eyes. "Not the kiss. The feelings, Boone. Have you two been dating without telling anyone? Because this looks pretty serious." She pointed her phone's screen at him. His spur-of-the-moment kiss on full display. Why had he kissed Violet? Hundreds of reasons. Because the moment had felt right, he had wanted to do so for a while now, and he had hoped it would help him sort through the confusion concerning what to do with his feelings.

Too bad it had only served to confuse him more. After the self-doubt he'd experienced at the rodeo he probably shouldn't have acted on his feelings but the fireworks and her closeness had done a number on him.

Boone dropped his head into his hands. "We're not dating."

"Then what *are* you doing?"

Boone shifted in his chair. "Honestly?" He raised his head again. "I don't know." He swallowed hard. "I care about Violet. She's…she's amazing." Images of Violet having fun with Hailey, joking with him around the campfire and how beautiful she looked in her dress and cowboy boots today sprang to mind. The other day he had convinced himself that any feelings he had for Violet were misdirected pieces of grief for his wife, but after their kiss Boone knew he wasn't just seeking friendly companionship with another person. It was Violet and Violet alone whom Boone craved being around. And not because he was lonely and grieving, but because he had fallen hard for the barrel racer.

Wade cleared his throat.

Evidently Boone was taking too long to supply an answer.

Boone met his brother's eyes. He pushed words past the tightness in his throat. "I think I'm in love with her."

Cassidy grabbed his hand and jiggled it. "That's wonderful. When I saw the picture, I hoped—but I wanted to make sure because I know Violet hasn't had the easiest life and I was afraid you might be leading her on. However unintentionally."

Boone rolled his shoulders. The kiss had been an instant reaction to her nearness, something he hadn't thought about beforehand. Hurting Violet was the last thing he ever wanted to do. He slipped his hand away from Cassidy and examined the lines crisscrossing both his palms. "Maybe this sounds ridiculous, but I keep struggling because it feels as if I'm not being faithful to June." His voice broke on her name. "I only just lost her. I don't deserve—I shouldn't find someone and replace her. I shouldn't get to be happy again so soon." He blinked hard. "It feels wrong."

Cassidy took his chin and lifted his head. "Boone," she said gently. "I understand what it's like to lose someone." She looked toward Wade. His brother's Adam's apple bobbed, causing the red-pink scar on his neck to move.

"For five years I thought Wade was dead," Cassidy said. "And I know it's not the same because I got Wade back, but I promise I understand how you're feeling and I know how complex and confusing it all can be." She dropped her hand to his chest, placing it over his heart. "You will always love June, but letting someone else into your life, being happy again and loving again, well, I believe your heart is big enough to hold all those emotions. Loving someone else doesn't negate anything you and June had."

Boone tried to absorb Cassidy's words but his worries still lingered. "I feel like I should wait. It's only been a few months since June—" Boone couldn't finish. He should suffer longer. Mourn his wife for a proper duration first. "The timing's all wrong and how I am right now, still processing everything, it's not fair to ask Violet to enter into anything with me until I'm through the worst of it, right?"

"Well, Boone." Cassidy flashed the picture again. "Looks to me as if the two of you have already *entered into something.*"

Boone sighed. He really needed to get a hold of her phone and delete that image.

Her eyes softened. "You don't have to meet some suffering requirement before being happy again, I promise you don't. No one would ask that of you, least of all June."

Wade moved to stand beside Cassidy and rested his hand on his wife's shoulder. She scooted on the coffee table to make room for him to sit beside her.

Wade steepled his hands, pressing them to his lips.

"Here's the thing, bro. Life has no certainties. Our family has had that lesson pounded into us a lot lately. In the last year we lost Dad and June, Alzheimer's stole our mother away, the ranch was leveled by a tornado, this happened." Wade touched the half circle scar on his neck, a reminder of his battle with thyroid cancer. "And now Silas. God's shown us Jarretts again and again that none of us are promised a tomorrow. There's no such thing as waiting for everything to be perfectly sorted out. Because the kicker is, perfect doesn't happen on earth, Boone. If you're waiting for the perfect time, then you're waiting for the impossible."

Wade took a deep breath and looked to Cassidy, seeking assurance. She put her hand on his knee. Their silent partnership wasn't lost to Boone. It made his chest ache. He missed having that.

"I'm no preacher and I've never been to seminary like you," Wade said. "But I don't think God intends for us to live in guilt and worry. From what I see in the Bible, we should be using our lives to chase after good things and pursue what God puts in our lives." Wade made eye contact and held it. "Are you so rich that you can shrug off a blessing from God? Because that's what this is, Boone. I know how you think. A relationship doesn't fit into your plans, your timing. But have you considered that God's timing is different than yours? If you have feelings for Violet—if you love her—you shouldn't feel bad about doing something about it. You should recognize her as the blessing she is."

Boone bumped his foot into his brother's. "When did my little brother go and get so smart?"

Wade gave the half smirk he was known for. "I have these two amazing big brothers that I've always looked up to." He shrugged. "I guess they've brushed off on me some."

Cassidy picked up her phone.

Boone shook his head. "Honestly, Cass, I don't need to see that picture again."

"It's not that. It's vibrating." She looked at the screen. "Rhett." She sprang to her feet and answered. "Does that mean—?" She gasped. "That's—that's wonderful. Oh, thank God." Tears clogged her voice and she paused. She held up a hand when Wade got to his feet. "Yes, of course. We will. I promise. All night." She gave her husband a watery smile. "Hey, Rhett? We love you guys. We love Silas. We're here for you any time, don't hesitate."

She hung up and turned to face Wade and Boone. Boone had risen to his feet, too.

Cassidy cradled her phone in her hands. She opened her mouth to say something and then her face contorted and she burst into tears. Wade had her in his arms a second later.

"I'm sorry," Cassidy got out. She wiped at her cheeks. "There's a heart for Silas. It's happening. Rhett wants us to call everyone together and pray while he's in surgery. The next few hours are critical." She faced Boone. "Go get Violet and we'll see if we can get through to Carter and Shannon."

Boone ran a hand over his head. He'd have to face

Violet before he had made up his mind what to do or say to her. He shoved away the thoughts swirling in his mind.

Silas was getting a new heart. For the next few hours a battle would be waged for his nephew's life. That was the only thing that mattered right now.

Chapter Nine

Violet tugged the sleeve of her oversize sweatshirt down over her fingertips as if maybe it could shield her better that way. It was a warm night but she had insisted on putting it on before heading to Wade and Cassidy's with Boone. Being here in the midst of the Jarrett family, watching them interact, she couldn't help but feel as if she didn't belong.

As if she was an intruder.

Knowing that Cassidy and Wade had seen the picture of her kiss made her uncomfortable, too. Had they laughed together over it? Or worse, pitied her? She wanted to make sure Cassidy knew that Hailey had sent the picture, but it wasn't an appropriate topic while Silas was in surgery or while Boone was in earshot.

Violet took a deep breath. She was here for Rhett and Macy, who had never been anything but kind to her. She was here because a little baby was in danger and his parents had listed her among the people they wanted gathered together praying. She would be here for them, no matter what anyone else in the room thought about her.

Cassidy pressed a fresh cup of coffee into her husband's hands, then she crossed to Violet, offering another. "It's the leaded stuff. Maybe it'll help with the long night." She set the mug on the coffee table where Violet could reach it. "I'd drink it, too, if I could." Cassidy laid her hand on her stomach.

Wade caught Cassidy's hand as she passed by and he gently wrapped an arm around her, drawing her onto his lap. "No one would blame you if you went to sleep."

Cassidy shook her head. "Even if I wanted to, which I don't—" She covered a yawn. The action brought a half smirk to her husband's face. "I couldn't if I tried. I'm staying awake until Silas comes out of surgery." She laid her head on her husband's chest. Coffee forgotten, Wade wrapped his arms securely around her.

Watching the loving couple interact caused a strong longing to wrench on Violet's heart. She looked away.

Back at her house when her phone had displayed Boone's name, she had thought—hoped—he was calling to talk about their kiss. But it had been something far more important.

Sweet Silas. The little superhero who needed their help tonight.

Violet pressed her hands together and prayed again, asking God to guide the surgeons as they worked and praying for Rhett and Macy as they spent the night clinging to a painful hope alone in a waiting room far from the rest of their family. Wade and Cassidy were whispering a prayer together at the same time. They had informed Violet that it was critical for the heart transplant to take under four hours to complete.

Kodiak was stretched out on the floor alongside the leather recliner Violet sat in. She reached down to scratch the dog behind the ears. Kodiak sighed contentedly.

Boone sat nearby at the kitchen table video-chatting with Shannon and Carter. "I know it's later for you guys there. We really appreciate you staying up with us. It's nice to be together, even like this." He gestured toward the laptop.

Despite the fact that it was two hours later in the Pantanal, a natural region of Brazil where they were currently located, Carter and Shannon both looked wide-awake. Carter wore a khaki shirt and had what looked like the strap of a camera bag still hooked on one shoulder. Shannon's blond curls were tucked in a bun and she had smudges of mud on her face and her shirt. As they spoke with Boone, whenever Carter glanced at his wife, he had a look in his eyes that said Shannon was the most beautiful, interesting person he had ever seen. He clearly didn't even notice or care that she had mud and dirt on her and neither of them looked as if they had showered recently. All they saw was the person they loved.

Violet's jaw clenched.

With his easy smile, chiseled jawline and black

hair, Carter was charming. When Violet had first met him, her interest had been piqued, but it had been clear from the get-go that the man was wholly focused on Shannon and only Shannon.

"It's no problem at all," Carter said. "We're actually used to being up most of the night. We've spent the last few weeks tracking jaguars."

"Tracking them?" Crossing his arms, Boone leaned back in his chair. They had been praying and talking about Silas for more than an hour and everyone was ready for a break. "For what purpose? I thought you were supposed to be doing veterinary work."

Shannon's hand slipped around Carter's arm. She studied him for a moment before turning to the camera, pride for her husband evident in her eyes. "It *is* important veterinary work, actually." She licked her lips. "We're on a working cattle ranch that also serves as a protected area for all species. Wild concept, I know, but it totally works. They have a thriving population of jaguars and pumas here. This program is helping the predators reclaim their numbers in this area. It's a really big deal."

Wade grunted. "Encouraging jaguars to live on a cattle ranch doesn't sound like a smart business plan to me."

Carter leaned forward. "But you'd be wrong and that's the point." He held up his hands. "Because they operate on a policy of total protection for all species, the prey population has boomed as well so the predators are far more likely to attack their natural prey than the cattle. The ranchers make a living without hurting the balance of this ecosystem—actually, the ranches are helping protect animals that would have been threatened by smugglers." His eyebrows rose as his voice rapidly picked up speed. "It's fascinating stuff. Can you imagine implementing something like this in Montana with the wolves or in locations where cougar populations have dwindled because of ranching?" He looked to Shannon, who offered him an encouraging nod. "When we get back…what I could do with what I've learned…the possibilities are endless."

Wade tilted his head. "Think about how much opposition you'll be met with here in Texas alone."

"We know. But this is important work." Shannon wrapped an arm around her husband's middle and leaned into him. "Not only is Carter going to be an amazing local veterinarian, but he's also set on helping native species reach healthy populations." They made eye contact and smiled in unison as Shannon said, "We're both committed to it and we have so many ideas."

Cassidy's phone rang and Wade helped her up as she answered it.

"It's Rhett." She accepted the call. "Can I put you on speaker?"

"Of course," Rhett's voice sounded through the room.

Ears perked, Kodiak sprang to her feet and ran a circle in the room. Each footfall was punctuated with a high-pitched whine. She started another loop and yelped, then went back to whining and pacing.

Wade reached for her collar. "If she keeps on like this, she's going to wake the girls."

"Kodiak, settle down." The second Rhett spoke Kodiak stopped, lay down and rested her chin on the floor. One last, long whine filled the room. "Good girl." Rhett's voice softened, wavered. "You're such a good girl. We miss you." His voice broke. "I'm so sorry we had to leave for so long." His breath rattled over the line. "Mace and I love you and it'll be okay."

Violet had risen while Rhett spoke. His words made a lump form in her throat and no matter how much she tried to swallow around it, she couldn't make it go away. She swiped at her eyes. While the exchange touched her, it also twisted her heart. No one had ever missed her or loved her as much as Rhett loved his dog.

A dog was more cared about, more a part of a family, than Violet had ever been.

Would probably ever be.

Macy came on the line. "We called because he's made it out of surgery, which is such a huge blessing already." Her voice sounded weary. "But keep praying for him because they said the next few hours and days will be precarious. He's far from out of the woods, but we're hopeful. We're trusting that God has big plans for Silas."

Wade pulled Cassidy and Boone into a hug with the laptop in the middle of them. Cassidy started to cry and Carter and Shannon cheered on their end of the call.

Violet took a step away.

She didn't belong here. Not any longer. She wasn't welcome in their moment.

As quickly as she could, Violet made her way to the door and soundlessly slipped outside. Taking the porch steps two at a time, she stifled a sob. The Jarrett family was everything she had ever wanted. A painful physical representation of what she had prayed for, begged God for and had never been given.

All she would never have.

Spending time with Boone today had been a bad idea. This was what happened when she let her guard down. Once again, it felt as if her hope had been used as a weapon against her.

Without thinking about her destination, she cut across the ranch property, hopping fences and skirting pastures full of cattle on her way through the Jarretts' vast holdings. She drank in lungfuls of sweet night air as she attempted to calm down. She had been alone all her life—she should be used to it by now. There were families in homes across the world who were just as warm and kind as the Jarretts, so there was no reason to allow the rejection of this one group to bother her so much.

So many families, yet not one had welcomed her in. Not one had seen worth in her.

Maybe because it wasn't there.

Ten minutes later as she climbed the hill toward the chapel, Violet had every intention of slipping inside and spending the rest of the night praying for Silas. That was until she passed the cross. She had avoided this area for weeks because the foster kids wrote what they were trusting God for on white rocks and left them at the foot of the cross on the Friday night of each summer camp session. By now, there was a gigantic pile.

Don't look. There was no reason to look.

But her gaze went there anyway. It couldn't help but trip over the rocks. One large rock made her stop in her tracks. The words there gutted her. *A Family.*

No one had cared enough to save her from pain, but in her own small way, she could rescue these kids.

Violet fisted her hands. She looked away from the rocks, up toward the sky. "Why do You do this?" she yelled. "All these kids." She flung a hand toward the rock pile. "All of them are counting on You to come through for them." She pressed her hand to her chest. "*I* counted on You and You didn't care, did You? Because for some reason I'm not good enough, not for You and not for them." Her gaze dropped to the horizon, where Wade's house was located. "Well, I'm not going to let these sit here—their hopes on display to only be let down." Violet sank to her knees. She made a sort of makeshift bag with the bottom of her sweatshirt and scooped rocks into it. When her bundle grew heavy, she rose and took one last look at the cross. "Well, You don't get these."

Then she headed down the hill, toward the lake.

After they hung up with Rhett, Boone glanced around the room. "Where's Violet?"

Trying to stem the flow of her tears, Cassidy fanned her face. "I'll check the bathrooms." She came back a few minutes later. Her lips bunched. "Did she leave?"

"I think she did," Wade said. He grimaced. "We left her out of that whole group hug situation. That couldn't have felt great."

A knot formed in Boone's chest. Of course that would have hurt Violet. He growled. Why hadn't he pulled her into their family embrace? He had been holding the laptop and excited about Silas being out of surgery, but he still should have thought about how it would affect her.

"Wait, what's going on?" Shannon called from the laptop. "I feel like we missed something big."

Cassidy crouched in front of the screen. "Boone's in love with Violet, but we don't know how Violet feels but I'm pretty sure I can tell how she feels from this picture I'm about to forward to you." She pulled out her phone.

"I'm going to delete that picture," Boone said.

"Too bad you don't know my pass code," Cassidy laughed and tapped away at her phone. He didn't know if it was the pregnancy or her joy over finally being married to Wade, but Cassidy had become close to all the brothers, to the point where she really fulfilled the lovable but annoying little sister role scarily well.

Shannon's eyes went to Boone. "What are you waiting for, you big lug? Go find her."

He looked to Wade, who just waved goodbye, dismissing him. Boone didn't wait for more. With Silas recovering and the Super Silas event only days away, he knew he would talk to all his siblings again soon. He grabbed his keys and headed to find Violet. His tires crunched as he drove the car slowly down one of the pebbled roads that crisscrossed the ranch. Boone scanned his surroundings, though this late at night it was difficult to make out much in the dark.

Why had she taken off?

God, help me find her.

Boone tugged out his phone. It had been on all day and was close to dying. But the easiest, most logical route usually was the best so Boone pressed to call her. It went straight to voice mail. Her phone had either died, she'd rejected his call or she had turned her phone off for the night. Any of the three was a viable option.

He scrubbed a hand over his jaw. They needed to talk—really talk and just be honest with each other. Because Wade was right—there would never be a perfect time to tell her that he cared, but she deserved to know. How would she respond? Boone hoped the kiss they had shared was his answer, but she could have been just as caught up in the moment as he had been. She might laugh at his declaration... Boone had never had to do this before in his adult life.

Tension crawled up his spine, around his shoulders.

He had to find her.

First, he headed to her bunkhouse. Everything was dark. What if she had simply been tired so she left? But that didn't sit right—Violet would have said good-bye. He knocked a few times, but there was no an-swer. Maybe she was tucked safely in bed and they could laugh about his frantic search in the morning, but for now he'd keep looking for her.

Next he went to the barn. Violet spent every free moment with Hawken so perhaps she had gone to see him before heading to bed. Upon entering, Boone went straight to Hawken's stall. The golden horse nickered when he drew near. Boone leaned over the edge of the half door, but Violet wasn't inside. He patted Hawken's side. "Sorry for waking you, buddy. I'll find her, go back to sleep."

Boone kicked at some straw on the ground and secured the barn again. He headed outside and stood for a few minutes, listening to the sounds of the ranch after midnight. Crickets, the windmill groaning near the cattle pasture, the hum of machines that kept the riding arena at a good temperature and the *plunk* of something heavy hitting water.

Boone craned his neck. Another *plunk*. The lake wasn't stocked with fish sizable enough to make that big a splash.

He headed toward the lake just off to the side of the horse pasture. The water wrapped behind Rhett's house and then meandered near the bunkhouses where Boone lived. It was the largest body of water at Red Dog Ranch. Surprisingly he hadn't heard the noise when he was over by Violet's house, but maybe it had only just started. When he crested the hill, Boone saw her. Violet had her back to him. She yelled something then hurled an object into the black water.

Relief flooded through his muscles, but it was quickly followed by worry. Violet had faced so many years of hurt. Boone knew she had been trying to trust God, but he also knew she had been through so much in her life, it would be understandable for anyone to struggle under the burdens she had faced. She tried so hard to be positive in front of everyone—to be who she thought they would like—but she never needed to plaster on a smile for his sake. He wished he could make her see that he cared about her no matter what. Since they first met, she had walked out on any conversation that touched a nerve or might cause her to break down. But he wanted her to know she didn't need to hide from him. Where he was concerned, she would always have a safe harbor to voice her doubts and fears and hurts without judgment.

When Boone reached the base of the pier, he realized what it was she was lobbing into the water. The rocks the foster kids wrote what they were trusting God for. Violet's shoulders shook as she held another rock up in the air. "You don't get this one either. Hear me? You don't get to crush this kid, too."

Oh, Violet. His whole chest ached for her and the pain she was clearly experiencing. He jogged down the pier, his steps causing the whole thing to groan and wobble.

Rock in hand, she spun toward him. "You shouldn't be here." Even in the dim light, he could tell her face was streaked with tears. The sight of her anguish tore at him.

"I wish you hadn't left, but I know why you did. It was thoughtless of me to leave you out." Boone wished she would yell at him instead of cry. Being railed at would have hurt less than seeing her tears. "I want you to know, you don't ever have to hide what you're thinking or feeling. Not from me."

"I think we both know you have better things to do tonight than be here with me." She tugged on her sweatshirt, pulling it tighter around her body. "You should be with that perfect family of yours," she said. "Not here. Go back to them, Boone."

He wanted to hold her, do whatever was needed to make her hurt go away, but first he needed her to see truth. Because it was clear to him that she believed his family was some out-of-reach ideal. She looked at them and saw all she didn't have. It was blinding her and causing her further undue hurt. Perhaps airing some of his family's dirty laundry would help her see that the Jarretts were simply people in need of God—no different from her.

"My family's far from perfect, Violet." He held his hands in a show of surrender as he edged a few inches nearer. "My dad wasn't very attentive with us kids, my parents lied to Rhett his whole life about being adopted and both my parents turned a blind eye on Wade when he was struggling with multiple addictions or when he spiraled so far out of control that faking his death seemed like a better option than facing his family." Boone took a deep breath and pressed on. "We all neglected Shannon to the point where she had to turn to an abusive man for attention, and then Wade didn't feel safe telling any of us he had cancer." Boone laid his hand on his chest. "Then there's me."

Violet still had the rock fisted in her hand. "Boone, you don't have to do this."

"I decided to become a minister because I figured that would get me some sort of gold stars with God." He had never admitted that to anyone before. Not even himself. "And looking back, I wasn't a very good husband. I failed June. I never asked what her dream was. We were married and I applied to seminary and then I told her we were going. I never even asked her if she wanted to go to Maine. I was incredibly selfish. And you saw what happened with Hailey."

She searched his eyes. "Why are you telling me this?"

"Because you're under the impression that us Jarretts are some ideal family unit, and that's just not true. We have made huge mistakes and have hurt one another in so many different ways." Boone laid his hand on his heart and shook his head. "Thank God for grace and forgiveness, because that's the only thing that's held us together. We've chosen to love each other through the ugly times. That's it." He exhaled. "The world is broken, Violet. That label extends to every person on earth. Especially me. We wouldn't need a savior if that wasn't the case."

She looked down at the rock in her hand. Turned it over and over. "Well, I'd take a messed-up family in a heartbeat over what I've got."

Boone held out his hand. "Violet, tell me what's going on." He reached to take the rock from her, but she moved her hand away. She paced back to the edge of the pier with the rock cradled in her hands.

She looked down at the word written there. *Love*.

"When I was a camper here your family made me write something on one of these rocks. Your dad." She glanced at him but it felt as if she was looking through him. "I wrote the same word every year. The same exact word." Her chin trembled.

Boone swallowed hard, meeting her gaze the whole time. "What did you write there?"

"Home," she whispered. She pressed her lips together and looked down at the rock. Her voice wavered as she continued. "Your dad told us that God cared, that He would answer our prayers, that He wanted to meet our deepest needs." Her fingers closed around the rock and a harsh laugh left her lips. "And you know, I actually believed him. I stupidly had faith that God would give me a home."

"It wasn't stupid." Boone took a step closer. "And God does care, Violet."

"Enough, Boone." She worked her jaw back and forth. "I'm setting this one free." She flung the rock far so it splashed into the lake. An owl hooted near the shore, seemingly offended by the disturbance.

There were more rocks piled by her feet. She bent to reach for another one. "They can stop waiting and hoping and trusting that someday someone is going to want them. They can stop waiting for someone to love them. Because it's never going to happen." Her voice broke and Violet's body sagged. "No one's ever going to want them." Boone wrapped his arms around her and pulled her so that her back was against his chest.

Boone kept her in a bear hug, his lips near her neck. "It's okay, Violet. It's going to be okay."

She pressed her hand over her mouth as her whole body trembled. "No one ever wanted me. They never—" She gasped for breath. "I trusted. I had faith. I *tried*, Boone. And look what it got me. I've never had a home." Violet turned in his arms, burying her face in his chest. "God didn't care enough to answer my prayer. And then when I had something good in my life, when I was climbing the ranks of the circuits, God took that away, too."

Boone held her as she cried. He would stand there with her secure in his arms all night if that's what she needed. So often people were uncomfortable around tears. That's what led people to say *stop crying*. But bottling his grief had only hurt Hailey and stunted his walk with God. He had learned his lesson. He wouldn't tell another to keep emotional displays to only things that made everyone comfortable. In fact, he could stand to learn from Violet in this arena.

Her tears ebbed, but she stayed with her head pressed against him. He would have pulled her even closer if it was possible. With Violet near, Boone's heart seemed to ram against his chest. Could Violet feel it? She had to.

"What am I going to do?" she whispered.

Boone licked his lips. "Stay, Violet. Stay here at the ranch." *Stay with me.*

"Stay?" She flattened her hands on his chest and looked up at him. The moisture in her lashes caught glints of moonlight and the sight undid him. How was it possible that she didn't understand how amazing she was?

She was wanted and always would be.

He bent, claiming her lips. How could she not think she had a place to call home when being near her had become the only home he wanted? Violet's body relaxed against his and he took the opportunity to deepen their kiss. Her fingers dug into his biceps, holding on as if his protection—his nearness—meant everything to her, and that's when he knew he couldn't go through life on autopilot anymore. Since their very first interaction, Violet had awakened in him a desire to live again. He wanted to feel; he wanted *this*.

With her.

Just as quickly Violet went rigid in his arms. She shoved against his chest, making him take a few steps back. His breath came out hard. She swiped her hand across her mouth and then held it out as if to warn him to keep back. Watching her, a heaviness filled Boone's chest.

How had it all gone so wrong? He had been about to tell her he was falling for her.

He rubbed his brow. "Vi—"

"I don't want you to say anything right now," she said. "You're too good at it. Your whole family is. You guys make everything sound too perfect and people like me fall for it." She took a deep breath. "I'm confused and all of this—" she moved her hands between them "—isn't helping. So you can't do that again."

"I'm sorry—"

She shook her head. "That doesn't help, either."

Boone swallowed. Everything he tried was wrong.

He wanted to tell her he was in love with her and they would figure this out. Ask her if she was willing to date a single dad who had never gone on a first date in his adult life. But as much as he wanted to spill his feelings, now wasn't the time. Her reaction to their kiss proved that. Right now, Violet needed someone to encourage her, to listen to her and to point her toward God. If he cared about her like he claimed to, then that's what he needed to do.

She met his gaze, her eyes narrowing. "Why do you want me to stay at Red Dog Ranch? This is your family home."

Boone prayed for the right words.

He took a tentative step closer. "Because this is where you belong, Violet. Anyone with eyes can see that. Rhett said it. Now I'm saying it. This can be your home, if you want it to be." Even if she never wanted to be with him. If they could only ever be friends. Boone would deal with it to have her nearby. He gently took her hand but left space between them. "What if God's answer to your prayers was *wait* because He had a home ready for you all this time? Maybe you had to wait because we needed you here."

Her lips parted as she listened and Boone had to remind himself not to kiss her again. She had said she didn't want him doing that anymore and he would respect that.

No matter how much he wanted to.

"God loves you, Violet. And whether your hope is mountain high—" he glanced at the pile of rocks and then the water "—or at the bottom of a lake. It doesn't matter, God still knows your heart." He jutted his chin toward the rocks. "You can dunk every single one of those into the lake, but it's not deep enough to escape God's love. Nowhere is."

It wasn't deep enough to escape Boone's love, either. But that wasn't what she needed to hear.

Chapter Ten

The next day, Violet was thankful that Wade had asked her to assess the new horses. Otherwise she would have been in the office with Boone, and she wasn't ready to face him yet.

Last night Boone had offered to walk her home but she had turned him down. He had seemed disappointed, but Violet had needed time to herself. As the memory of both of their kisses flooded her mind, she hugged the stack of papers that made up the horses' pedigrees and medical forms to her chest. After the Fourth of July celebration she had convinced herself that Boone had been caught in a moment, but after their embrace on the pier she couldn't just write off his attention.

Was it possible that Boone Jarrett cared about her?

Boone had just lost his wife. He was a man who had been with the same woman since high school. And while Violet believed Boone to be the most honest and genuine man she had ever met, it made sense that he would confuse friendship for something more. He was lonely and Violet was the only available woman near his age working at the ranch.

It wasn't *her* he wanted. Just someone, just comfort. Maybe he had convinced himself otherwise, but Violet figured he would change his opinion as he healed from the loss of his wife. He would find someone more suitable to one day be a pastor's wife at some quaint church. A woman who spent the night flinging symbols of a bunch of children's hopes and dreams into a lake and who shouted at God probably wasn't fit for that sort of role.

She entered the riding arena and took a deep breath. Horses, dust, fresh wood and leather—all smells that comforted her. Riding was the only real home and constant she had ever experienced. The arena had pristine riding sand and the barrels Violet had set up a week ago were still in place. She had started walking Hawken through the course. Whenever she did, she noticed he moved with a bit more pep.

The indoor arena had been Shannon's dream. In the spring, she and Carter had raised the money needed to finally build the large structure. It held a full-sized arena, tiered benches lining the two long sides to accommodate a few hundred onlookers and an area in the back end where horses could wait indoors for their turn. Violet trailed her fingers over the top of the wall that protected the onlookers from the action. It was a significantly nicer arena than some of the ones she usually practiced in. In time, the ranch would utilize the space to hold riding lessons for foster children and host their own rodeo events.

The six horses Wade had picked up at an auction were tied along the western wall of the arena. She ran her hands over the first horse, checking to make sure it had been brushed and was clean before she started tacking it. Satisfied, she began to saddle the first horse. The mare pawed at the ground when Violet started to tighten the cinch, so she stopped to let the horse get comfortable before continuing.

"Shhh." She stroked the animal's powerful neck. "You're safe. This is your new home." She swallowed hard. Boone had basically said the same things to her. But Violet couldn't forget Cassidy's text. Boone was close to his family and because of that, Violet was sure he wouldn't want to be with someone long term that his family wasn't excited about. Moreover, Violet didn't want to be with him when he realized that he didn't really care about her.

When he realized she wasn't enough.

If she stayed at the ranch, they would have to remain just friends. It was the only way.

But after yesterday, she didn't know if that was even possible.

She finished saddling the first horse and ran her through a series of tests, then Violet worked her way down the row. A rotund brown gelding named Puddin' walked about as fast as a sleepy sloth, and on the other side of the spectrum there was a roan named Maverick who would require an incredibly experienced rider. The final horse on the line was a gorgeous dapple-gray named Disco. Violet approached him, running her fingers along his back. She had read over his papers three times, not believing what she saw. He was older than Hawken, but he was a trained barrel racer. Her body all but vibrated with excitement as she took him on a walk and then a canter around the edge of the arena. Disco veered toward the barrels twice.

It wouldn't hurt to run the barrels once.

But one time turned into ten turned into fourteen. She let him rest but he quickly turned back toward the course, hungry to go again. Disco flung sand in an arc as he dug toward the barrels, and he moved with a frenzy and drive that Hawken hadn't yet attained. They charged down the finish line one last time and Violet tossed her arms out, threw back her head and whooped. Her heart pounded in her ears as adrenaline left her legs tingly. She had missed this. Missed it so much.

Someone clapped in the seating area, making Violet jump. She pivoted in the seat to see Boone rise to his feet, giving her a standing ovation.

He had been at the top of the tier, but he started to make his way toward the half wall. "I have to say, that was captivating. I mean, I knew you were a champion, but Violet, you were amazing."

Violet steered Disco toward where Boone stood. "It feels weird to run it with someone other than Hawken. But this guy's a good horse." She rubbed Disco's lower neck.

Boone rested both of his hands on the edge of the

wall. He tilted his head. "It's not all him. What you do out there, it's a gift." He shot out a breath, his eyebrows going up at the same time. "I have to admit, I was wary about your racing. It's such a dangerous sport."

Disco adjusted how he was standing and let out a huff.

Violet swung down from the horse. "The danger factor is half the reason people like to watch the barrels." She started to lead Disco back to where the other horses were. Boone rounded the half wall to walk beside her. "I hope this isn't your attempt at convincing me to stop." Because she wasn't about to.

"Not at all," Boone said. "Just trying to say you've gained a new fan."

"Really?"

"What I just watched?" Boone let out a low whistle. "It was impressive. Terrifying, but impressive."

Violet snorted. She and Disco hadn't been going anywhere even close to full speed. After all, it had only been her first time riding him. But she had been able to feel how much more he would have given if she had pushed him. She wondered how he would do under the less ideal rodeo conditions where the stress of the crowd and poor ground conditions forced the horse and rider to depend on each other far more. With time and trust, Disco could become an incredible, prize-winning horse for some rider.

Boone held out his hand, letting Disco nuzzle his palm to take in his scent. "You know, there's still a lot of the circuit left this year." Boone kept his eyes on the horse. "Couldn't you enter with this horse?"

Violet's nails bit into her palm as she gripped Disco's reins. "You think I should leave here? Go back to the circuit?"

Boone patted Disco's neck. He finally met Violet's eyes. "I do, Violet. There's no denying where you belong."

Violet's throat felt thick as she snapped her attention back to Disco.

Boone wanted her to leave.

There was her answer. No more confusion. No more wondering.

She focused on unlacing Disco's cinch so she could tug his saddle and blanket off as quickly as possible. She hadn't ridden any of the horses for long so she felt comfortable choosing to brush them later, after Boone left. She stepped around Boone, heaving the saddle onto the railing. Then she slipped off Disco's bridle, replacing it with a halter. Despite trying to act as if she was fine, her movements were jerky. Telling.

There's no denying where you belong.

Not here. Not with him.

All his kind words last night—the offer that Red Dog Ranch could be her home—more Jarrett false hope. More lies. She should have known better. How many times would she have to get bitten by her own misplaced hope before she learned her lesson?

Apparently, she was a slow learner.

Violet forced herself to breathe steadily and evenly. She had to keep it together until she was away from

Boone. He had rejected her like everyone else in her life had. But his dismissal tore her in two in a way the rest of them never had—because she had believed he was different.

She had allowed herself to fall in love.

Violet's eyes burned as she led Disco to a holding pen where the rest of the horses were waiting.

Boone trailed after her. "Did I say something wrong?"

After Disco was safely tucked in the pen, Violet closed the metal door with more force than necessary. A loud clang echoed through the cavernous building. "Actually, you said exactly what I needed to hear." He was standing so close, she brushed shoulders with him as she passed.

"Violet, stop, please." Boone lightly caught her by the arm. "You're clearly upset."

She shrugged out of his hold. She needed him away. Needed to push him out of her life so he couldn't touch her heart again. "Let's not do this."

He cut into her path. "You walked away from me on day one, you did it twice on the pier, at Wade's house and I know you almost walked out on me the first time we had a bonfire." His voice was pleading. "Stop running, Violet. Stay and talk to me."

It was the *stay* that finally caused her anger to boil over.

Violet whirled on him. "You have no right to accuse me of anything. *I'm* not the person who decided his own child was too much of a burden to be around for two whole months." Boone flinched, but

Violet pressed on. She jabbed a finger in his direction. "This whole time you've hidden away, keeping your struggles from your family so they could keep seeing Boone the spiritual leader who can fix all their issues and never has problems of his own. Well, I've got a wake-up call for you. Whether or not you want to admit it, you're drowning in problems. And pretending you're not just makes you a fake like everyone else." Violet fisted her hands at her sides and set her shoulders. "I'm not the only one who walks away from hard things, Boone."

He reeled back. "I encourage you to ride and this is how you respond?" He grabbed at his hair. "I'm trying, Violet. I'm really trying but—"

"You want me to up and ditch Hawken." The muscles in her arms quivered. "To take some other horse and go back to the rodeo just so I can be out of your hair."

Boone put his hands in a *whoa* gesture. "I said nothing remotely close to that."

"Hawken is my family. My only family." She jabbed her finger in the direction of the horse barn. She didn't have the veterinarian's approval to transport Hawken in a trailer yet or else she would have gone and packed him up right that second. "Just because you're fine with ditching the people you supposedly care about whenever it's convenient for you, don't assume the rest of us are like that."

Boone pressed his fist to his lips and closed his eyes. His shoulders rose with a large inhale. "Is this about Hailey? Because I admitted I was wrong,"

Boone said. "I completely messed up, but I've made changes."

It was so hard to stay mad at Boone when he sounded so sincere, but if Violet was going to protect herself, she had to. Because no one else seemed concerned with protecting her heart.

"What about when you take off for school in the fall? The second summer's over that will be your priority and she'll go back to second place." Violet worked her jaw. They had spoken once about seminary and she had encouraged him to pursue local options but he had never brought it up again. For all she knew he was headed back to Maine next month.

Boone's brow bunched. He opened his mouth but whatever he was about to say was cut off by a little girl's earsplitting wail and the loud *bang* of a door. *Hailey.* Boone broke into a sprint, tearing across the large arena to try to catch his daughter. Violet was only seconds behind him.

Whatever Hailey had heard had been too much.

Violet had intended to push Boone away with her caustic words.

Instead she had broken a little girl's heart.

Boone hurled the heavy front door of the arena open and quickly scanned the area for his daughter. Bright sunshine momentarily blinded him. Shielding his eyes, he squinted and glanced at each of the nearby fields. His chest rose as his breaths came hard and fast. "Hailey," he called. "Hailey, sweetheart, where are you?" He stalked to one side of the arena and looked for her there, then checked the other side. No Hailey.

His gut rolled. Where was she?

Sweat slicked the back of his neck, his temples.

She only had seconds on him. She couldn't have gone far.

He called her name again. Then another time.

Violet shoved through the door. "Did you find her?"

Boone scrubbed his hand over his jaw. He couldn't look at Violet. Not without saying something he'd regret. He didn't know why she had insisted on picking a fight, but whatever her reasons, she had gone straight for the jugular and he wasn't okay with that. He shoved his fingers through his hair. How had it gone from attempting to show support for something she loved, from encouraging her dream, to her yelling at him?

"Don't worry," Violet said. "I'll help you find her."

Boone stalked away, his back to her. "I think you've done enough already."

"I'm sorry she heard." Violet's voice was so small, it did funny things to his heart.

But his daughter was scared and crying somewhere because of Violet's careless words. Because Violet had let her fear and emotions control her and overcome sound reasoning. He thought they had been to the point in their relationship where she would trust him enough to be honest and to be able to tell him what she was thinking.

Apparently, he'd misread a lot of things lately.

Boone's jaw hurt from clenching it. "Sorry she heard, but not sorry for saying it?"

She looked away.

Well, now he knew.

Since his first week back at the ranch Boone had been trying to help Violet, trying to be there for her and draw her out. He had done everything in his power to assure her he was a safe person who cared for her. That she could be gut-level honest with him without fear.

But none of it had mattered, had it?

Looking back, Boone had made a right fool of himself.

Violet had chosen to push him away too many times to count. If she wanted to keep her guard up, there was nothing he could do to change that. Only she could choose to change and decide it was time to grow and trust people. And she wasn't ready. At least not when it came to him.

He knew that now.

Boone shook his head. Hailey needed to be his focus; she should have been his main focus all along. Since coming home to Red Dog Ranch, Boone had allowed his attention to be too divided.

Maybe Hailey had headed back to their bunkhouse. It wasn't that far away and she could have reached it by now. He'd check there first.

"Boone." Violet was a few steps behind. "She has panic attacks. We need to find her."

He rounded back on her. "What do you mean, she has panic attacks?"

Violet wound her fingers together. "She told me when we were on the Ferris wheel." She looked down at her hands. "She said she's had them since her mom died. She has a hard time breathing when it happens and—"

"And you didn't think this was important to tell me before now?" Boone growled as he turned and looked toward his bunkhouse, then back to the barn. He didn't know where to go. But with anger mounting inside his chest, he knew he had to get away from Violet. What he was feeling wasn't all Violet's fault, but their current interaction wasn't helping matters.

The image of Hailey hiding somewhere, hurting and struggling for breath, completely gutted him.

Panic attacks. Had he been blind to his sweet daughter's struggles? Boone's heart sank. The back of his throat ached and it felt as if he was going to be sick. He so badly wanted to be the father Hailey needed, but he kept failing her.

He would never get this parenting thing right. Not without June.

A wall of grief crashed through him, threating to drop him to his knees.

Move, Boone. Do something.

He started toward the house but changed his mind at the last second. Twisting, he bashed his hip against the fencing near the arena. A lance of pain shot through his body. Boone huffed out a breath, biting down the harsh words he was tempted to unleash.

Regrouping, he jogged to the horse barn, which sat lower and in front of the riding arena. Boone shoved open the rolling doors. A loud sob caused his pace to quicken.

"Hailey." Boone strode down the row of stalls. His little girl was in here somewhere. The sound led him to the stall Hawken occupied. He spotted Hailey inside. Relief made his legs wobbly and he grabbed for the framing around the stall door for support. His daughter's tiny arms were wrapped around one of the horse's front legs and her face was shoved into his shoulder. Her body shook with a series of loud cries. Hawken had his head bent low so the side of his chin rested against her back. If Boone didn't know any better, he would have said the horse was hugging Hailey.

Boone slipped into the stall, dropped to his knees and pulled Hailey onto his lap. Their movements caused a swirl of straw dust to float around them. Immediately, Hailey spun and tossed her arms around his neck. Hawken nickered low, his hot breath washing over them.

"Don't go, Daddy. Please don't go again," Hailey cried.

She buried her face against Boone's neck, her tears slipping down the back of his shirt. Ever so carefully, Boone inched his way out of Hawken's stall. Hawken had always been a gentle horse, but he wasn't taking chances where his daughter was concerned. Out in the hallway, he took hold of Hailey's shoulders and set her so he could meet her gaze.

"I'm not going anywhere, Hailey. Do you hear me?" He smoothed his hand over her hair, then bent forward, pressing a kiss to her forehead. "I love you and I'm so sorry I left you here after Mom's funeral. That was so wrong of me. Dads make mistakes, but I promise I won't do that again." He took her small hands in his. She was so vulnerable and he promised himself he would protect her and be there for her however she needed for the rest of her life. Boone thanked God for entrusting her to him. He asked for God's grace and guidance.

Hailey's face contorted and she started crying harder. "First Mommy left us, then you left me for a long time." Her gaze snapped to something over his shoulder. "I don't want Violet to leave us, too."

Boone's knees dug into the cement, but he wanted to stay at his daughter's level for the conversation. He framed Hailey's face with his hands, drawing her to make eye contact. "I'm only worried about you right now. Our family is you and me, remember?" She nodded and sucked in a rattling breath. "You don't have to worry about our family being separated ever again because Violet was wrong, sweetheart. I'm not going anywhere. No one and nothing could make me leave you." He brushed his thumb across her cheeks, gathering up her tears.

Hailey's lip trembled. "I miss Mommy."

Boone wrapped her in a bear hug and for the first time since finding out about June's accident, Boone let himself cry in front of Hailey. Maybe he had been wrong to hide his grief, to fake a strong facade. He had chosen to do so for her benefit—so she could look to him as someone solid in her life instead of seeing her dad falling apart. But he had done her a disservice by not inviting her into his grieving process; he had made her feel like she had to face her fears all alone.

"I miss her, too. Every single day." Boone's voice was hoarse. "I loved her so much."

Surrounded by horses and straw and dust motes, they clung to each other and cried together. When they finally stopped, Boone scooped his daughter into his arms and carried her back to their bunkhouse.

"Hey, Dad?" Hailey's hot breath trailed over his neck. Her fingers touched the hair at his nape. "I love Violet, too."

"I know." He sighed and decided to be completely honest with her. "I feel the same way."

Hailey sat back a little so she could see him. She pursed her lips and lowered her brow. "Then how come she isn't part of our family?"

"Because sometimes love isn't enough to save somebody," Boone said carefully. "They have to decide to love themselves first. They have to choose to accept your love, and I don't think Violet can. Not yet."

Maybe not ever.

"Well, I'm going to keep loving her. I'm not going to stop. And when she's ready, my love will be right here." She touched her heart.

Boone's chest felt hollowed out as he glanced toward Violet's bunkhouse. He hadn't stopped loving Violet, either, but it was time to put Hailey and her needs first. Even if that meant sacrificing what he felt for the most beautiful barrel racer he'd ever met.

Chapter Eleven

Violet finished packing her belongings an hour before she had to be at the Super Silas event. After everything happened with Boone and Hailey yesterday, she had made a phone call to Wade and had solidified her plans. When she had asked Wade not to tell anyone, he had given his word but had warned her that in his experience, the truth was always the best option.

Despite his advice, she had decided to leave Red Dog Ranch.

It was best for everyone.

Well, everyone but Hawken. But Wade had promised he would be cared for. Carter would personally work with her horse once he and Shannon returned from their veterinary mission trip and they would let her know the second Hawken was cleared for transport. Once that happened, she would take him with her and never look back.

No matter how much doing so would hurt.

The fact was, she had started to imagine a place

for herself at Red Dog Ranch, but after seeing how much she had hurt Hailey, she couldn't stay. In Violet's pursuit for a home, she had been selfish—she had hurt a child and had inflicted pain on Boone, too. Even though she knew she loved both of them more than she had ever loved anyone else in her life, she had still been willing to say horrible things in order to push them away. Maybe Violet wasn't cut out for relationships after all. Perhaps that's why God hadn't ever allowed anyone to stay in her life.

Besides, with June's death still so fresh, Boone and Hailey were already dealing with enough without adding Violet's baggage into the equation.

Our family is you and me, remember?

Violet had stayed long enough to hear Boone say that to Hailey. And he had been right. All the same, it had stung to be left out. And the anguish in Boone's voice when he had said he loved his wife had been so clear.

How could Violet have ever believed Boone would want to be with her when he was still so obviously in love with his dead wife? From everything Violet had heard about June Jarrett, it sounded like she was near perfect, whereas Violet was a broken person who had nothing to offer their little family. Nothing but more heartache. Who would welcome that?

No wonder Boone had suggested she should leave the ranch. He had seen her on Disco and seized an opportunity to make a clean break.

Violet looked up at her truck's ceiling and blinked until the burning sensation in her eyes faded. She was doing the right thing. She had to get out of their lives before she caused more damage to really good people. Before the realization that she would never measure up sank any deeper into her bones.

Violet checked her hair in her truck's rearview mirror, took a deep breath and then headed into the Chick-N-More. Thankfully the place was buzzing with activity and she was given a task the second she walked through the doors. Boone was there, and so were Wade and about eight other people they seemed to be friends with. Piper, Hailey and Cassidy weren't there yet so Violet assumed they must have been together.

After assessing what needed to be done, Violet went to her truck to gather the box of jars she had decorated for the superhero voting. When she turned and headed back toward the restaurant, Boone was waiting by the front door.

Her heart squeezed at the sight of him. Boone was so handsome and his presence spoke of protection and care, but she couldn't think about those things.

He cleared his throat as he pulled the door open for her. "About yesterday…"

Violet shook her head. "Today is about Silas."

Boone nodded and followed her inside. They parted ways immediately; he headed to the cash register area so Patrick could run him through the ordering process while Violet set to work decorating the voting area. Last night she had found one more large jar to add to her collection. She had put a picture of baby Silas on it and labeled it *Super Silas*.

She placed it in the center of the table and fanned the other jars around it.

As they worked, people started lining up outside the restaurant and by the time the doors opened, the line filled the parking lot, snaked down the street and continued around the next block. Country music pounded through the speakers and Violet set to work taking people's orders, delivering food and answering questions about how Silas was doing. Rhett and Macy had recorded a video that played on a loop on a large screen near the voting area and pictures of Silas filled the walls.

After a quick break, Violet headed to her next table but when she saw who was seated in the booth, she froze in the middle of the walkway.

Cassidy, who had arrived with the girls when the event opened, came up alongside her and placed a hand on her lower back. "You okay?"

"I can't serve that table," Violet said.

"They asked for you by name. They said they heard on the news and saw in our flyers that you would be here." Cassidy eyed her. "Who are they?"

Violet swallowed hard. It was the Jenningses. "They were my foster family. Mrs. Jennings taught me how to barrel race."

Mrs. Jennings looked up from the table and caught Violet's eye. The older woman's hair had grayed in the last few years, but other than that she looked the same. Her old foster mom gasped and rose to her feet. "It's really you," she said, stepping toward Violet. "Is it okay if I hug you?"

Violet nodded and Mrs. Jennings didn't skip a beat. She tucked Violet into her soft embrace. "Child, how I've missed you." She took Violet's hand and led her back to the table. Mr. Jennings and the two youngest of their six children sat with them. Everyone got up to hug Violet and then they ushered her into an empty seat. Mr. Jennings slid what looked to be a large photo album toward her.

Mrs. Jennings batted at his arm. "That's embarrassing, Mark. Don't ask her to sign it just yet."

"Sign what?" Violet knew she was probably wide-eyed, but she had never expected to see the Jenningses again, let alone hug and visit with them.

Mrs. Jennings smiled nervously. "Maybe it'll sound silly to you, but we've kept a scrapbook of everything you've done over the years." She opened the book and showed the articles and news clippings that were glued inside. They had recorded all of her accomplishments. Another page had pictures of Violet with them when she had lived with their family. "We're so proud of you."

Violet flipped through page after page. Mrs. Jennings had taken the time to write little notes for each entry. Violet blinked back tears and her throat felt thick. "I don't understand. Why would you keep all this? If you cared this much, why didn't you adopt me?" The last part had slipped out, but now it was out there.

Mrs. Jennings took hold of Violet's hand. "We wanted to, and we've regretted not saying something to you sooner. But we had six kids and all the horses to care for and we were accepting other foster children." Her smile was sad. "We meant to talk to you, tell you we wanted you to stay and be a part of our family, even if it wasn't formal. But we never got a chance." She tilted her head. "Why did you take off in the middle of the night like you did? By the time we tracked you down you were a rising star on the circuit and we figured you wanted nothing to do with us."

Not wanting to be a burden, Violet had left the Jenningses' house a few days after her eighteenth birthday. "I didn't think you wanted me."

"We did, Violet." Mrs. Jennings squeezed her hand. "We still do, actually." She exchanged a glance with her husband. "Maybe it's too late, but we would love to reconnect with you and—" She looked to her kids, who both made a *hurry up* motion. "And ask you to start doing things with our family again, if you'd welcome that."

For the rest of the evening, Violet kept looking back over to the table where the Jenningses were seated, as if to make sure they were real.

They had wanted her.

This whole time.

Would her life have played out differently if she hadn't run off that night?

Violet would never know.

She had told them she would take them up on their offer and they could see what happened from there. Of course, she wouldn't live with them again or truly act like one of their children, but after everything, at least she knew there were people in the world who loved her.

That's all that mattered, right?

The hollow feeling in her heart gave the wrong answer.

Howard waved at Violet from across the packed room. Ryker was at his side, a model service dog. When she saw Rhett again, she'd have to let him know how well his first trainee was doing.

If she ever saw Rhett again.

Violet rubbed the back of her neck.

Boone led the room in a time of prayer for Silas, then he pulled numbers for a raffle Patrick was hosting. Everything that was up for grabs had been donated by Chick-N-More. Violet reminded herself to eat here more often.

Then it hit her once again that she wouldn't be in the area much longer. Only for quick visits with the Jenningses and whenever there was a nearby rodeo.

When it was her turn to take over the mic, Violet rounded up the jars and declared Super Silas the winner of the best superhero competition. Everyone in the room burst into cheers. Violet searched the sea of faces for the one that she knew would calm her nerves, the one who would make her comfortable. The set of eyes that had become home to her.

She found Boone across the room. Sound fell away as they made eye contact and for a heartbeat, it was just the two of them and she wondered if, despite everything, they could make something work. If anyone ever asked, she would never deny that she loved

Boone Jarrett. Loved him enough to do what was best for him and Hailey. Leave without complications, without burdening their life anymore. Leave before she hurt them more than she already had.

She snapped back to attention when people began pounding on the tables. She was supposed to give the wrap-up talk.

Violet forced a smile. Hopefully they couldn't tell that she was breaking apart inside. Because walking away from Boone was the most difficult and painful thing she had ever done.

She thanked everyone for coming, then took a deep breath. "I also wanted to announce that I'm officially rejoining the rodeo circuit. For my first race back I'm going to enter the jackpot race and any winnings I receive will go directly into the Super Silas fund." This time when she scanned the room, she made sure to skip over where she knew Boone was stationed. "So if you happen to make it out to the show, stop by and cheer me on."

As the event ended, people surrounded her. They kept congratulating her and asking her to sign things for them. Some promised they would attend her next run or they would look up her schedule now that she was back in the circuit. The Jenningses walked outside with her and she hugged down the line of them. Mrs. Jennings made her settle on a time for a phone call in the next week and then they headed on their way.

When Violet turned toward her truck, Hailey blocked her path.

Hailey pursed her lips. "I thought Hawken was hurt."

At the sight of the little girl, a ball of emotion lodged in Violet's throat. Violet tried to swallow around it, but doing so made her chest ache. "Your uncle Wade said I could borrow Disco for the season." Violet planned to head back, hook up her trailer, load up Disco and leave before anyone else returned. "It was actually your dad's idea." A sad little laugh escaped from Violet's lips. "He wants me to go back to the rodeo. And he's right, it's time."

Hailey eyed her.

"I have to go." Violet's voice wavered. "How about one more hug, squirt?"

Hailey raised an eyebrow, but obliged. "Why are you acting funny?"

Because I don't know if I'll ever see you again.

Violet ran her hand over the little girl's soft hair. "Just know that I love you so much, okay? Don't ever question that."

Hailey's eyes went to something behind her so Violet pivoted to see what she was looking at. Boone. He was smiling and shaking hands with people on the other side of the parking lot.

Violet reached for her truck's door. She had to get out of there but she also didn't want Hailey to ever have to question things or wonder like Violet had at her age. Violet took a deep breath. "Your dad is a good guy, Hailey. The best guy. And he's working so hard to be the dad you need, okay? Sometimes that means making hard choices and sometimes that

means things might happen that you don't like or understand, but just know he loves you and I love you
no matter what. Does that make sense?"

The little girl quirked an eyebrow. "How about my
dad? Do you love him?"

Violet couldn't help the tears that gathered in her
eyes. "Yes," she whispered. She wouldn't lie to Hailey. "I'll always love your dad, too." She laid her hand
on her chest. "You will both forever have a home in
my heart. Don't ever doubt that." She would turn into
a blubbering mess if she stayed any longer. So she
jerked the door open and climbed inside. "Be good,
squirt."

Hailey backed away from the truck and waved
goodbye.

As she drove away, Violet glanced in the rearview
mirror a dozen times or more, each time wondering if
this was the last glimpse she would ever have of the
two people who would always hold her heart.

When Violet hadn't shown up at the office the
next morning, Boone had chalked it up to a late
night. Maybe she was sore or had to work extra with
Hawken. There was a chance Wade had asked for
more help with the new horses as well. But when
Violet hadn't made an appearance by noon, worry
started to gnaw away at any focus Boone might have
had before.

They hadn't talked—really talked—since their
argument in the indoor arena. And there was still so
much awkwardness between them from what had

happened on the Fourth of July. After Hailey had overheard them fighting, Boone thought the best thing for her was to focus all his attention on his daughter. But when he prayed about it, he had realized that Violet had become important to both him and Hailey so he needed to get to the bottom of what had upset her so much the other day. For the present, he prayed he could be the friend she needed without pursuing more. Boone sighed. He would hope for more one day, but for now, it would be enough to know Violet was in a good place and was continuing to heal after all she had endured. He would keep healing, too, and maybe someday be able to gain her trust.

Her phone went to voice mail and texts went unanswered. Why did people own phones if they never had them on?

Boone worked his jaw back and forth.

He wanted to tell her how proud he was of her for deciding to use Disco in the rodeos. Riding someone other than Hawken had to have been a difficult choice for her. But her joy in the arena the other day had been palpable. It was important to Boone that she knew he fully supported her choice to pursue something she so clearly loved doing. Boone had never had that moment with June, so he wasn't about to miss doing whatever he could to be there for Violet's dreams.

When the front door of the office finally opened, Boone practically pounced. But it was Wade, not Violet, who stood in the entryway.

Wade gave him a half smirk. "Don't look so disappointed to see me."

Boone shoved his hand through his hair. "I just thought you were going to be Violet."

"Now I get why you're disappointed." His little brother winked in an exaggerated manner. "She's much prettier than me, though I'm not so bad."

Boone snorted. "*Much* is an understatement."

Wade suddenly sobered. He cocked his head as his eyes narrowed. "She didn't tell you." He turned to the side, rested his hands on his belt and blew out a loud stream of air. "Wow, I can't believe she didn't tell you."

"Tell me what?" His brother wouldn't meet his eyes. "Wade?" He practically growled his name.

"Violet's gone, Boone." Wade hooked his hand on the back of his neck. "Like, gone, gone."

"You mean she left for the rodeo?" Boone spoke slowly. "I was there last night. I heard the announcement." Although Boone hadn't thought that meant the very next day, but even if it did, she would go to the event and then come right back. Red Dog Ranch would be her home base. They'd established that, hadn't they?

Wade grabbed Boone's shoulder, offering a squeeze. "She left for good, Boone. She asked me not to say anything to you at the event but I figured that was because she was planning on telling you in person afterward." Wade scuffed the toe of his boot against the ground. "That she would at least say goodbye. I promise, I tried to convince her to change her mind or at least give it a few days before making a decision."

"But she'll be back, won't she?"

Wade shook his head. "After the event she came back here to load Disco into her trailer. She told me she was going to have to drive through the night to hit the next location on the circuit. It didn't sound like she had any intention of returning."

Boone blocked out whatever Wade said next. He wouldn't listen until he had proof. He sidestepped his brother to get out of the office and then broke into a sprint, heading toward the horse barn. She wouldn't have left Hawken behind.

Hawken is my family.

She would never leave that horse.

Boone shoved into the barn and strode directly to Hawken's stall. The horse lifted his head and nickered. With a sigh, Boone's muscles relaxed. He held a hand out to Hawken, who instantly flooded his palm with his warm puffs of air. For a minute, Boone rested his forehead along Hawken's long nose. He'd never been a big fan of horses, but Violet loved this one so Boone had learned to do the same.

He heard Wade's labored breaths not far behind him.

"If he's here, she's not gone." He stood up straighter and stroked Hawken's neck. "Not for good."

Wade came up behind him and laid a hand on his shoulder. "Sometimes people do have to make the hard choice to leave behind the ones they love. Sometimes they think it's for the best or they convince themselves they had no other choice." Boone knew Wade was speaking from experience. His younger brother had faked his own death, abandoning his entire family for five years before resurfacing. The whole time Wade had believed it was better for everyone if he wasn't in their lives.

Wade's sigh sounded like it cost him something. "Boone, she packed up her bunkhouse and returned the key. It doesn't get much clearer than that. She's gone."

"Who's gone?" Hailey's voice caused both men to turn toward her. Piper had her cat cradled like a baby in her arms and Hailey stood next to her. Boone had forgotten they often played around the barn together when Cassidy was tied up in the kitchen.

Boone rolled his shoulders. The reality that Violet left without saying goodbye made his chest feel hollowed out. Now he had to tell Hailey that they had another loss to face together. "Violet's gone, Hailey. She doesn't live on the ranch anymore."

Hailey quickly shook her head back and forth.

Boone took a knee in front of her. "It's going to be okay." He reached for her.

Hailey shoved his hand away. "This is your fault. This is all your fault." Her voice shook. "You told her to take Disco and leave."

"No, sweetheart." Boone kept his voice calm, belying the storm of emotions churning through his chest. "I didn't tell her to leave." He reached for her again and she stepped back, the motion twisting his insides. "Hailey, remember, our family is you and me and we're going to get through this. I promise."

Hailey's tiny hands balled at her sides. "You're

wrong. Violet's our family, too. She told me." Hailey pounded on her chest as her tears flowed. "She said we live in her heart. That's family, Dad. That means *we're* her family." Hailey's little face screwed up. "Don't you like her? She wouldn't go unless she thought you didn't like her."

He had loved her and it wasn't enough. But that wasn't something he thought Hailey could comprehend. "Sometimes grown-ups just have to leave."

"No," Hailey said loudly. "She said she loved you. She told me, Dad." Hailey's shoulders shook as she wiped her eyes. "Why did you let her go?"

Boone's mouth opened, then closed. When had Violet said all of these things to Hailey?

Did it matter?

Violet had run from Boone since day one and he had made a fool of himself pursuing her. She had pushed him away every chance she had gotten. And when the opportunity to leave the ranch had arisen, it seemed as if she had jumped at the chance to hightail it away from him.

If he stepped away from his feelings where she was concerned, Boone could even accept that her leaving was for the best. What had he been playing at, falling for someone like Violet? Violet lived an exciting and fast-paced life, and he was a book lover who would rather stay home. She had a career that kept her traveling, and Boone and Hailey needed roots and family. Boone was on course to become a pastor—so despite what was in his heart, Violet wasn't an option for him. Besides, Violet's career choice was dangerous. Boone had already lost someone he loved, so it was best not to completely fall for someone he could lose so easily again.

She was gone and it was for the best.

Maybe someday he'd actually believe that.

Chapter Twelve

Two weeks had passed since Violet left Red Dog Ranch. In that time she had donated two jackpot wins to the Super Silas fund, so Boone assumed she was doing well. This week closed out the last week of Camp Firefly and while Boone had enjoyed working with the campers, he was relieved it was almost done. Boone had gotten used to running the ranch and the camp sessions on his own, but he missed working alongside Violet.

He just missed Violet. Period.

Rhett had called a few days ago with the good news that Silas's recovery continued to go well and it was looking as if he would be released from the hospital sometime soon. They would then have to stay within thirty minutes of the hospital for six weeks before finally coming home. It would be autumn before Rhett, Macy and Silas were back at Red Dog Ranch. Shannon and Carter would be back from South America by then, too, and Wade and Cassidy's baby was on track to be born around the same time. The whole family would be together.

Yet someone important would be missing.

Boone shook that thought away.

That weekend after the last of the campers left, Boone decided to roam his family's property while he prayed by name for each of the foster kids who had spent time at the ranch that summer. He carried a list with him and worked his way down it one by one. He prayed for God to work in their lives and prayed for their futures.

Soon after Violet had left, Boone had decided he had two choices: mope or use his energy toward things that mattered. He had chosen the latter. Deciding to view the foster children at the ranch through the lens of understanding Violet had afforded him. He had kept her in mind while he reworked his chapel messages, making sure to balance out hope with truth and offer tangible ways to deal with what felt like unanswered prayers and broken dreams. He also made sure he addressed how to combat feelings of unworthiness.

He often ended up at the cross near the little chapel where he prayed over the words the kids had written on their rocks. However, while he made his way up the hill today, he noticed two people standing near the cross. It was the weekend and most of the ranch's staff had left for their day off. No one besides his family was expected on the property today.

The man and woman huddled together. The woman bent to lay a bouquet of cheerful yellow flowers at the foot of the cross, then she turned into the man's shoulder and loudly started to cry. Boone had no desire to disturb such a moment, but he did need to see what they were doing at the ranch. His boot crunched on the path and the couple glanced his way.

"Sorry," Boone said. "I didn't mean to intrude. But I live here and I wanted to see if I could help you."

The woman pulled a wad of tissues from her pocket and dabbed at her eyes. "We didn't mean to encroach, either. It's just, we met as campers here." Her chin quivered as she looked to her husband.

He cleared his throat. "We both grew up in the foster system and we met here." He tipped his head toward the cross. "We met God here, too, and that changed everything." He brushed hair from his wife's face. "We were married at this chapel. Your dad walked her down the aisle to me."

The woman nodded. "Then we had a baby." The last word was distorted by a sob. She covered her face and held up her other hand. "I'm sorry. I need a minute."

The man wrapped his arm tighter around his wife. "Our son didn't make it." His Adam's apple bobbed. "We donated his organs and given the timing and location we're pretty sure his heart saved Rhett and Macy's son."

Boone's mouth went dry. He scrubbed his hand over his jaw. Boone had faced losses in his own life, yet he still wasn't sure what to say. Grief was so individual in how it worked. "I'm so sorry for your loss."

The woman dabbed at her eyes again. "You're the brother who lost his wife, aren't you?"

Boone laid his hand on his chest. He wasn't surprised that they knew. Many of the foster families kept up on the Jarretts and the ranch. "Yes, ma'am, I am."

"Then you get it." She offered him a watery smile. "I wanted to be so angry with God. Sometimes I still am. I think I'll struggle with that for the rest of my life."

Boone nodded. "I understand." Sometimes he was still angry with God for taking June, for the miscarriages they had grieved during their marriage and over what had happened with Violet. "Believe me, I do."

She rested her hand on the cross. "But then I remember, God lost His son, too." She trailed her fingers over the chipped white paint. "He experienced the same loss and pain and brokenness that we're feeling. He understands it all more intimately than any parent ever should."

A slight breeze trickled over the hill, making the yellow flowers wobble on the pile of rocks. In an effort to alleviate the tightness in his chest, Boone crossed his arms. In the midst of his grief, he had never considered God's loss or realized that God had faced the same pain. It had been easier to blame God than seize the opportunity to understand Him more.

The man took his wife's hand. "We were talking on the drive here about how when Jesus was on earth, everyone in the Bible had a plan for him. They thought he would sweep in and save them from their oppressors in a physical sense. But God's plans for His son were different. He saved everyone, but in a much more powerful way. On Palm Sunday, none of them knew that Easter Sunday was coming or what it would mean." He coughed a little to cover the emotion that was clearly evident in his speech. "Just like that, we had so many plans for our son's life, but God had a different plan." His shrug seemed almost painful. "I guess what I'm trying to say is it brings us comfort to know that his heart will always be at Red Dog Ranch, because this place holds such significance for us."

The woman wrapped her hand around her husband's arm. "And we're believing that this means God has amazing plans for baby Silas. Please let your brother know that we're going to pray for him for the rest of our lives."

"I will." Boone was completely humbled by their strength and bravery. "I have to say, you two have amazing clarity in this situation."

The woman reached out and squeezed Boone's arm. "If our Zachary were still fighting for his life it would be different. If we still had hope of having him in our life, we would be doing everything we could to keep him. But we don't, so our hope is in finding the next step in all this and finding the good we can."

"We should head out." The man gestured toward a cherry-red car parked near the office.

But the woman still had a hold of Boone's arm. "You have a sweet little girl, don't you?"

"I do."

"Life is so precious. I pray that you'll live that way instead of living in defeat and in grief. See the blessings God continues to place in your life. Pray the same for us, too." She squeezed his arm. "God has so much more for you, Boone Jarrett. Are you brave enough to believe that?"

Long after the couple left, Boone stayed on the hill near the cross. The couple had shared so much wisdom with him and he had never even asked their names.

Life is so precious.

If we still had hope...we would be doing everything we could to keep him.

God has so much more for you, Boone Jarrett. Are you brave enough to believe that?

After Violet had left, Boone had gone back to living his life in a numb autopilot way. He was going through the motions but he wasn't feeling anything. Even in the moments when he looked up the location for her next race or when he checked her standing in the circuit, he would tell himself that a rodeo rider and a minister could never be together. He had convinced himself that it was pointless to go after her because a life together couldn't work.

But what if they could?

While he still had the hope of a chance with Violet, he should fight for a life together. It was foolish to sit around in defeat. Life *was* precious, and no day should be taken for granted.

He was done wasting time.

Boone headed down the hill.

He needed to find Hailey and they needed to look up Violet's schedule.

The roar of the crowd hammered through the entire rodeo arena as the rider in front of Violet finished her run. From her waiting spot, Violet scanned the crowd for familiar faces like she had done at every rodeo since leaving Red Dog Ranch. Her stomach plummeted until she spotted Mr. and Mrs. Jennings on the bleachers waving at her. She smiled and waved back.

At least she had someone there who cared about her.

Violet patted Disco's neck.

Actually, that was wrong. She didn't only have the Jenningses.

In the time since she had returned to the circuit and had reconnected with the Jenningses, Violet had finally realized that God had been there all along. She had prayed for a home and family when she was younger and God *had* brought both of those things into her life. She had failed to recognize what God had done because her ideal looked different than the true gifts He had placed in her life all along. The rodeo was her home and the Jenningses had always cared. Weeks ago, she had prayed for God to hold her, failing to see that He had been holding her safe and secure for her entire life.

She wouldn't lose sight of that again.

The arena suddenly fell silent.

Her turn.

Working her bottom lip between her teeth, Violet ran a hand over the smooth rawhide cantle of her saddle. Tension laced the air like smoke after gunfire. Disco shifted beneath her.

"You're fine, boy." As Violet trailed her fingers over his shoulder, her catapulting stomach began to soothe. Disco knew the barrels. They had been placing well with each run.

The announcer's voice snapped Violet to full attention. He read off a string of her accomplishments and told about her accident early in the season. While he talked, she mentally practiced the cloverleaf racing pattern.

Keep centered. Visualize the set. Leave a clear pocket.

The official nodded to her.

With a defined kick and the lift of the reins, Violet gave Disco his head and he erupted forward, slamming her into the saddle with a jerk that rattled her teeth. Charging down the alley of the rodeo arena, horse and rider busted through the center entrance at Mach speed. They crossed the electronic timer beam and tore toward the first barrel.

Violet couldn't help but smile. Their approach was dead-on. She fought against a laugh.

Picking Disco's speed at the precise moment, she arced him, leaving a good pocket to give him an even turn. He swung around the orange-and-blue painted barrel, his hooves digging into the loose ground. Anchored in the saddle, Violet clenched her abs, her right leg pressing along Disco's rib cage for support. Half clawing the rawhide horn, she looked through the turn toward the second barrel. Raising the knotted reins in her sweaty hand, she allowed Disco to rocket forward across the arena, kicking up a mixture of sand and dirt in his wake.

Clocking left around the barrel, they jolted forward, pounding toward the final one with electric force. She and Disco hugged the last barrel with practiced accuracy, then turned and let loose down the straight. Violet kicked wildly and Disco galloped toward the finish, crossing the timer.

As the race ended, the real world rushed back in. Applause echoed down the arena's corridors. Violet's muscles zinged with adrenaline as Disco clip-clopped down the cement hallway. She guided him outside to cool down. The smells of manure, leather, popcorn and animal sweat hung together in the late-summer air.

Squinting against the sunshine, Violet shielded her eyes. When she was able to focus, her gaze landed on a handsome man with short cropped hair and a tiny blonde girl waiting just outside. Boone and Hailey. Violet's heart pounded wildly.

Hailey bounced up and down waving her arms. "Violet. Do you see us? We're right here."

Boone made eye contact with her and didn't let go.

Violet's heart rammed into the back of her throat. She swung off Disco's back and led him over to where the pair were standing.

Wade appeared behind them. "How about I take Disco?" He lifted the reins from her hands. "I'll get him untacked and brushed down." He jerked his head toward Boone. "You've got more important things to focus on."

Hailey launched toward her, hugging Violet around the legs. "I missed you so much."

Violet hugged the girl tightly. "I missed you so much, too."

Hailey jumped back and pointed at her dad. "He missed you tons. Tell her, Dad."

Boone rubbed at the back of his neck. "She's right. I've missed you every day. I wish you would have told us you were leaving."

"What are you doing here?" Violet asked. Today's rodeo was a four-hour drive from Red Dog Ranch. Not that Violet calculated the distance from the ranch for every rodeo. Who was she kidding? She did it every time. "Boone?" She searched his face.

Boone's brow creased. "Red Dog Ranch has been my home for my entire life. Even when I was in Maine for school, I thought of the ranch as home. But the truth is, it hasn't felt like home for weeks now. Not without you there." He swallowed and took a step toward her. "I don't want to be there without you, Violet." He rested his hand on top of Hailey's head. "Neither of us does."

"That's why we came," Hailey said.

"But I hurt you both so much." Violet looked away, across the fairgrounds, and focused on nothing in particular. Guilt over making Hailey cry and over the horrible things she had said to Boone still ate at her. "You two have been through so much already." She shook her head. "You don't want to add my baggage to all that, Boone. You don't."

Boone gently took both her hands in his. "This amazing woman once told me that the people who love you aren't ever going to see you or your struggles as a burden." He lifted her hands to his chest. "And we love you, Violet." He rested his hands on hers, capturing them over his heart. "I love you."

Violet blinked away tears. "I love you, too," she whispered. "I'm so sorry I hurt you. I'm so sorry for how I left. I didn't want to but I thought it was for the best."

"I know. We forgave you a long time ago. I hope you can forgive us for taking so long to come after you." Boone let his hands slip away, then he nodded to Hailey. The little girl pranced back to a bag they had left behind them and pulled out a white rock. She handed it to Boone, who held it out to Violet. The rock had one word painted on it. *Loved.*

"I know you haven't always been a fan of these white rocks."

Violet pressed her fingers over her lips. "There are a bunch at the bottom of the lake that can attest to that fact."

Boone's chuckle was adorably nervous. "Well, these aren't hopes. These are promises." He tugged her hand away from her face so he could set the *Loved* rock on her palm. He curled her fingers so they wrapped around it. "You are loved," Boone said. Hailey handed him another rock. *Wanted.* "You are wanted." Boone set the rock into Violet's other hand. Hailey pulled another rock from the bag. *Home.* Boone added that one to Violet's pile. "And you will always have a home with us."

When Hailey went back to the bag a fourth time Violet laughed through her tears. "How many rocks do you have in there?" She was so touched by Boone's gesture. He had replaced the thing that had been a symbol of her shattered childhood hopes with tangible truths. She was loved, she was wanted, she had a home.

Violet would keep these rocks forever.

Boone's grin turned sheepish. He licked his lips. "Just one more." Hailey handed him the rock, but this time Boone didn't immediately give it to Violet. He cupped it between his hands so she couldn't read what was written there. "This rock's a little different. We could say this one is my hope...one only you can turn into a promise." Then he got down on one knee and held the rock out to her.

Marry Me?

Violet gasped. The three rocks she already held clattered together in her hands. "I don't know what to say." In a much quieter voice she added, "I'm not June. I'll never be the wife you lost." She knew saying such a thing could end the most romantic moment of her life, but she had held her tongue waiting for the right minute far too many times with Boone. She wouldn't do that again. If they were going to be together, she was going to always be honest with him about her doubts and fears. It was the only way they could ever be a healthy couple.

"I'm not asking you to be." Boone released a shuddered breath. "Violet Byrd, I love *you*. From the moment we met you have made me feel alive. You have challenged me and made me reexamine my life and my relationship with God in a way no one else has ever done. You are kind and good and you are already an amazing role model to Hailey. I want you in my life and in Hailey's life because of who you are and no other reason. I have never seen and will never see you as a replacement for what I lost." He shook his head. "You're the precious gift that I never expected but will cherish forever if you'll let me."

Violet took the rock from his hands and cupped the four she had to her chest. "What about the rodeo? Where will we live?" Doubts spilled out of her. The idea that Boone wanted to marry her despite all their ups and downs seemed unbelievable. "I'm not exactly preacher's wife material."

Boone quirked an eyebrow. "Is it all right if I stand up to keep talking? This ground is hard and my knees aren't as young as they used to be."

Violet nodded.

Wade rejoined them and took Hailey by the hand. He led her away so Boone and Violet could be alone.

Boone rose. He tucked a strand of hair behind Violet's ear, then left his hand there to cup her face. "You love the barrels and I will never ask you to give up your dream. I'm going to start taking seminary courses at a slower pace at a school near the ranch. It'll take longer to complete my degree, but I'll have more time for the people I love and I think that's important right now." He smiled. "Some of the courses are even online so I can complete them from anywhere. Like, for example, on the circuit." He shrugged.

She opened her mouth but he plunged forward.

"You once mentioned that the rodeo doesn't have a church. That believers have to seek out each other in order to experience any sort of community," Boone said. "What if we started a ministry for rodeo riders? Hailey and I could travel with you during the circuit season, which only lasts a few months. I can homeschool her if that's what needs to happen. We'll be there to cheer you on and I'll find a way to minister to people while I'm beside you." He eased the rocks from her hands, set them back in the bag, then returned to take her hands again. "We'll figure out a way to make it work and all be together because you're worth it, Violet."

Her heart pounded out a double-time rhythm. She wanted to shout *yes* and jump into his strong arms but there was still one more thing they needed to address. "What about the danger, Boone? Riders can get seriously injured or worse. After what you've been through, that's a valid concern."

Boone pressed his forehead to hers. "I made peace with that when I realized it's far more dangerous for my heart to live without you."

"Boone." Violet bit her lip. "Why haven't you kissed me yet?"

Boone tossed back his head and laughed. The sound flooded Violet's chest with warmth. How she had been able to convince herself to walk away from him was beyond her understanding. If she had it her way, she would never be away from this man again.

"Because a month ago you told me you didn't want me to kiss you anymore," Boone said. "So I'm not going to do it until I get your okay." He leaned so close their noses brushed for a second, his breath mingling with hers. Violet sucked in a sharp breath. He was teasing her, being so near. The man knew exactly what she wanted and what he was doing. She loved him all the more for his ability to be playful in the midst of an emotional moment.

"Why haven't you answered my question yet?" he whispered.

Marry Me?

Violet inched closer, her lips grazing his. "My answer is yes." Then she looped her hand on the back of his neck and tugged him down for a kiss. This time when a little girl cheered, they didn't break apart. Instead, Boone wrapped his arms around Violet and lifted her off her feet to kiss her even more.

Epilogue

Thanksgiving

Hailey hugged the pan of s'mores bars to her chest and smiled up at Violet as they walked toward Rhett and Macy's house. "Everyone is going to love these. I know I do."

Violet winked at Hailey. "They'll all just be really happy your dad didn't make his famous mashed potatoes." She jabbed Boone in the ribs.

Boone slung his arm over Violet's shoulders. "Hey, now. I know the difference between a cup and a tablespoon now." He laughed.

Violet sighed in a joking way. "It was a teaspoon, honey."

Hailey adjusted how she was holding the pan so she could take Violet's hand. "Can we go for a family ride tomorrow?" Violet and Hailey had started riding horses together every morning but Hailey always wanted her horse-shy daddy to join them.

Boone grimaced. "What horse would you guys stick me on?"

Violet waggled her eyebrows. "How about Maverick?"

"How about no," Boone said. Even busy with schoolwork and his plans for establishing a rodeo ministry, Boone had heard all about Maverick's wild antics. Out of all the staff, only Violet had been able to ride him so far.

They walked up the steps to the large ranch house as one unit. Hailey broke away to knock on the door.

Violet leaned against Boone. "Actually, I would put you on Puddin'."

Hailey wrinkled her nose. "But he's that old one that falls asleep on the trail."

Boone pointed at his daughter. "Oh, now he sounds perfect." He bumped his hip against Violet's. "You know me so well." She snagged a kiss from him and he went in for another one a heartbeat after they parted. Violet's heart soared.

The door to Rhett's house swung open and they were greeted by the scents of roasting meat, baked goods and spices. Boone sniffed the air and groaned like a hungry bear.

Macy welcomed them in. "And the lovebirds have arrived," she announced. "The party can officially begin."

Hailey handed Macy the pan of s'mores bars. "Am I a lovebird, too?"

Macy tweaked her nose. "Of course you are. Because everyone here loves you so much."

Hailey trotted off to find Piper. Piper lofted her

gray-and-white cat in the air. She had dressed him up in a turkey costume. "Look, Cloudstorm loves this. Getting dressed up is one of his favorite things." Cloudstorm did not, in fact, look like he enjoyed playing dress-up but thankfully he was a very patient cat. He pawed at the turkey headpiece tied over his ears. Then when Piper was distracted with fixing his headpiece, Cloudstorm snatched a few loose feathers from the ground and took off running.

The house buzzed with conversation. Carter and Shannon were visiting with Cassidy in the kitchen. Rhett and Wade were nearby, Rhett holding Silas and Wade holding newborn baby Grace. Kodiak sat at attention beside Rhett, her eyes never leaving the bundle in his arms. They had even received special permission from the memory care facility for Mrs. Jarrett to join the family for the holiday. She sat at the table, watching over all her children with a wide, wistful smile on her face.

Violet walked over to Rhett and Wade. She touched Grace's tiny fist. "She's so beautiful."

"Takes after her mom that way." Wade winked.

Piper snorted. "She may be cute but you should know that she is very, very loud."

Wade and Cassidy exchanged an amused look. Cassidy mouthed *I love you* at her husband and then went back to adding the last details to their food.

Carter joined their little circle. "Hawken looked great out there today." He shoved his hands into his pockets. "As long as we don't push him too hard, I don't see any reason why we can't start putting him through the course with you on his back. We should be right on track to have you guys back on next year's circuit."

Boone's arm brushed against Violet's when he joined their group. "I agree. He looked awesome out there today." He turned toward Violet. "Have you decided between him and Disco yet?" She had been debating which horse she should enter next year and was torn. She loved Hawken, but she didn't want to chance causing him any more injuries. And Disco was incredibly devoted and loved to run the barrels. Then again, Hawken had started this journey with her and it didn't feel right replacing him. They had discussed giving Hawken to Hailey—that way he would be loved and in the family, but there wouldn't be a risk of him being injured in a competition. But Violet was still mulling it over.

She shook her head.

"No worries," Boone said. "We'll figure it out. Either way, both those horses are going to be well loved." He rubbed his hands together. "And speaking of well loved, can I hold that nephew of mine?"

"That would actually be great," Rhett said. "Then I can help the ladies get all the food on the table." He started to hand Silas to Boone. "But fair warning, Kodiak is going to watch you like a hawk as long as you're holding him. Don't take it personally—she does it to me, too."

"Rhett isn't kidding. She's become Silas's ever-present protector," Macy called from the kitchen. "I'm afraid she's ditched Rhett for a more handsome little man."

Rhett ran his hand over his son's head. He pressed a kiss to Silas's temple. "I wouldn't have it any other way."

"Here." Wade passed Grace into Violet's arms. "I better go help or my wife will insist she's fine to heft that huge bird to the table on her own and Rhett's too nice to defy her so it's going to have to be me." Cassidy had given birth five weeks ago, but during the first week she had been admitted back into the hospital with a uterine infection. Since then Wade hadn't been willing to take any more risks when it came to the health of the woman he loved. Violet couldn't blame him. Sometimes Cassidy could be too stubborn and self-sufficient for her own good.

Wade donned bright pink oven gloves and removed the turkey from the oven with a flair only he could pull off. "Looks good." He sniffed. "Smells good, too." He set the bird on the top of the oven and Cassidy brushed him aside so she could ladle the juices over the top and add finishing touches.

Wade glanced at Shannon. He thumbed toward the turkey. "Are we sure this isn't your goose?"

Shannon smacked her twin across the chest. "Not funny."

Carter chuckled. "I can attest to the fact that Wing Crosby is very much alive and well. He followed me around all morning." Carter's phone started to ring. He apologized and tugged it from his back pocket. He had let the family know he was on call at the veterinary clinic in town so if someone had an animal emergency he would have to leave. His face drained of color when he saw the name on the screen. His eyes found Shannon's. "It's my sister."

"Take it. You have to take it." Shannon shooed him out of the room.

Mrs. Jarrett coughed, making everyone in the room turn her way. "Well, I don't know who that is." She gestured toward Carter's retreating form. "But I sure don't mind having him around because he's one very handsome man."

Shannon crossed to her mother and took her hand. "Mom, that's my husband, Carter. You've met him before."

Mrs. Jarrett's whole faced bunched up as if she were working a math puzzle. Then she looked at Shannon. "If that's so, then, child, you are a very blessed woman." Their mother grinned.

Shannon's eyes grew huge. "Mom," she said, turning the one-syllable word into three.

"What?" Mrs. Jarrett shrugged. "I may be old but these eyes still work, you know."

When the whole family finally gathered around the table, Violet ended up between Boone and Mrs. Jarrett.

Rhett stood at the head of the table. He took the time to meet each of their eyes. "Our family has endured our share of heartbreak these last few years. Even still, or maybe because of it, we have so much to be thankful for." Macy grabbed his hand.

Mrs. Jarrett's hand found Violet's. "It's so nice to have our whole family together, isn't it?" She patted Violet's arm. "It's so nice to be home."

Violet laid her other hand on Boone's knee and she bent her head as Rhett prayed over their meal. At one point she peeked around the table, and the sight of so many people she loved gathered together made her heart expand.

Her family.

Next month she and Boone would make that official at their wedding, but these people were already a piece of her and always would be. They were imperfect and goofy and loving and she wouldn't change a thing. They had managed to draw closer as a family while they had weathered incredibly difficult things. And there was no doubt they would see hard times and go through more struggles in their lives, but Violet knew this family was strong enough to get through anything because they loved one another and they loved God.

When the prayer ended, Violet pressed a kiss to Boone's jaw.

He grinned at her. "What was that for?"

"Because your mom's right." Violet shrugged. "It's nice to be home."

* * * * *

Enjoy all of the books in Jessica Keller's Red Dog Ranch miniseries:

The Rancher's Legacy
His Unexpected Return
The Wrangler's Last Chance
Starting Over in Texas

Available now from Love Inspired!

Dear Reader,

I don't know about you, but I'm a little weepy about leaving the Jarrett family. I have loved getting to know these characters. I hope you've enjoyed getting to know them, too.

When I first started Boone's story, I began to question if I had taken on too much. Boone *just* lost his wife. Surely he wouldn't be ready to fall in love again that quickly. And Violet's a mess (and that's putting it nicely!). How on earth was I going to get these two to their happily-ever-after? But God is known to rebuild in the midst of ashes, and time and again in the Bible He blessed and used people who weren't perfect, who doubted and who—by the world's standards—weren't ready. He uses people just like Boone and Violet. Just like you and me.

I hope you enjoyed reading Boone and Violet's story as much as I loved writing it. If you enjoyed this visit to Red Dog Ranch, make sure you pick up the other books in the series—there's one for each sibling.

Thanks for reading!
Jess Keller

AN AMISH MOTHER'S SECRET PAST
Green Mountain Blessings • by Jo Ann Brown

Widow Rachel Yoder has a secret: she's a military veteran trying to give her children a new life among the Amish. Though she's drawn to bachelor Isaac Kauffman, she knows she can't tell him the truth—or give him her heart. Because Rachel can never be the perfect Plain wife he's looking for...

THE BLACK SHEEP'S SALVATION
by Deb Kastner

A fresh start for Logan Maddox and his son, who has autism, means returning home and getting Judah into the educational program that best serves his needs. The problem? Molly Winslow—the woman he left behind years ago—is the teacher. Might little Judah reunite Logan and Molly for good?

HOME TO HEAL
The Calhoun Cowboys • by Lois Richer

After doctor Zac Calhoun is blinded during an incident on his mission trip, he needs help recuperating...and hiring nurse Abby Armstrong is the best option. But as she falls for the widower and his little twin girls, can she find a way to heal their hearts, as well?

A FATHER'S PROMISE
Bliss, Texas • by Mindy Obenhaus

Stunned to discover he has a child, Wes Bishop isn't sure he's father material. But his adorable daughter needs him, and he can't help feeling drawn to her mother—a woman he's finally getting to know. Can this sudden dad make a promise of forever?

THE COWBOY'S MISSING MEMORY
Hill Country Cowboys • by Shannon Taylor Vannatter

After waking up with a brain injury caused by a bull-riding accident, Clint Rawlins can't remember the past two years. His occupational therapist, Lexie Parker, is determined to help him recover his short-term memory. But keeping their relationship strictly professional may be harder than expected.

HIS DAUGHTER'S PRAYER
by Danielle Thorne

Struggling to keep his antiques store open, single dad Mark Chatham can't turn down his high school sweetheart, Callie Hargrove, when she moves back to town and offers her assistance in the shop. But as she works to save his business, can Callie avoid losing her heart to his little girl...and to Mark?

LICNM0620

LOVE INSPIRED
INSPIRATIONAL ROMANCE

UPLIFTING STORIES OF FAITH, FORGIVENESS AND HOPE.

———————

Join our social communities to connect with other readers who share your love!

Sign up for the Love Inspired newsletter at **LoveInspired.com** to be the first to find out about upcoming titles, special promotions and exclusive content.

———————

CONNECT WITH US AT:

Facebook.com/LoveInspiredBooks

Twitter.com/LoveInspiredBks

Facebook.com/groups/HarlequinConnection

LISOCIAL2020